Protecting Vidalia

Brandy Golden

Published by Brandy Golden Books, 2023.

PROTECTING VIDALIA

First edition. February 24, 2023.

Written by Brandy Golden.

Chapter 1

The Whippoorwill hooted its low rhythmic tones into the starry night as Vidalia Ann Minton dragged her heavy suitcase out of the passenger's side of the four-wheel drive pick-up truck and then looked around. The tones of the whippoor-will were haunting, making her feel uneasy.

Some legends say the whippoorwill hoots when a death is imminent. If so, they were a little late, she thought. Death had already placed its cold finger in the fabric of her life and changed everything.

Placing a mental lock on that thought, she concentrated on the storm coming in. The wind in the pine trees was picking up, urging her to get inside as quickly as possible.

Vidalia had packed plenty of provisions in the back of the pickup, enough to last several days, maybe even the entire two weeks she'd planned to be here if she wanted to stay that long. She was still undecided about that, but this spot was about as far from civilization as she could get.

Just what she needed.

She grunted as she tugged the heavy, soft-sided luggage up the wooden steps and over to the door of the cabin and then fished in her pocket for the key. Swearing softly, she wiggled it around inside the keyhole impatiently until it finally opened. The sense of urgency to get inside was escalating as the low growling of thunder rumbled across the heavens. "Thank God," she muttered as she felt for the light switches on the inside of the door jamb.

The soft glow of a yellow bulb lit up the murky evening above her head with the first switch. The second switch sent light beyond the open doorway, challenging the creeping darkness. Heaving a sigh of relief, Vidalia stepped into the beckoning stillness and out of the whipping wind. The protection was short-lived as she set her suitcase down and headed back to the truck to get her food supplies.

By the time she brought in the last load, the inky blackness of the Rocky Mountains had closed in around her, and the small oasis of light burning from the cabin's interior was extremely appealing. She shivered as the cool evening air nipped at her slender arms in the short-sleeved t-shirt. She should have worn jeans, she reflected, but back in Fort Collins this afternoon, the denim shorts had been perfectly reasonable.

After shutting the door against the brisk winds behind her, she leaned back against it, the box of canned goods crushed against her chest, and closed her eyes. The approaching storm was creating anxiety that led to things she didn't want to think about. "Compartmentalize," she muttered to herself. "Getting settled in is the priority at the moment." As usual, her mind didn't want to cooperate. Taking a deep breath, she walked to the kitchen area, set the box of canned goods on the small table, and began inspecting her surroundings. The first thing she did was turn the heat up on the thermostat.

When her friend Dax had offered her the use of his cabin, she'd jumped at the chance, desperate to get away. She needed to think, to figure out where she was going with her life, and most importantly, how she was going to forget the horror of one awful night.

Shuddering as the memories tried to close in on her, she plugged in her stereo and stuffed in a copy of Neil Diamond's *Coming to America* CD, then began to rummage around for kindling in the wood box to start a fire. Music was always a distraction for her and a fire in the fireplace always felt good. Both spoke to her soul in so many different ways.

Her friends all thought she was crazy for liking an old geezer like Neil Diamond. After all, that was her grandmother's time. Vidalia was only twenty-three and Neil Diamond was old enough to be her grandfather.

She loved it though.

In fact, she loved a lot of the seventies and eighties music, feeling a kinship with Rod Stewart's *Tonight's the Night* and Lionel Ritchie's *Dancing on the Ceiling*. It was feel-good music, as her mother always said, and in her young opinion, it lived up to its name. She turned it up as loud as her ears could stand—anything to drown out the intrusive memories and the increasing windy fingers making the glass rattle in the patio door and around the windows.

The cabin wasn't huge, but it had a loft upstairs with a couple of beds, one bedroom downstairs, and a huge fireplace in the middle of one wall. The downstairs area was open to the kitchen. A small table and chairs sat near the patio doors to the wrap-around deck, and a nice, light brown leather sofa with matching recliners adorned the living area.

The huge beams above her head looked like knotty dark pine, and the floor was done in the same wood. The walls were painted a deep creamy color. The huge fireplace on one wall with bookshelves on either side and the plush tan rug between the sofa and the fireplace gave the cabin a cozy, homey atmosphere.

A large screen TV hung above the fireplace. Dax had told her there were movies in the bookshelves or she could bring some of her own if she wanted to. She'd brought a few of her favorites, although she wasn't sure how much television she would be watching. Hiking and photography were a huge interest of hers and she intended to spend as much time outside as the weather would permit.

As the trees outside the windows dipped their branches in deference to the wind, Vidalia was thankful she'd made it in ahead of the gathering clouds. It had looked like rain all afternoon on the drive in from Fort Collins and air had started cooling the minute she'd began her ascent into the mountains.

The flames were just shooting up from the kindling and catching on the bigger sticks when a horrendous pounding began on the door. Startled, Vidalia whirled around, her heart rate increasing dramatically. Who in God's name would be out in the middle of nowhere in the dark? She hadn't heard a vehicle in the driveway and surely no sane person would be on foot in this weather. Quickly, she sped to her purse and took out her pepper spray, her hands shaking badly.

All the stories she'd heard about being confronted by a stranger raced through her head. She picked up her cell phone. The commercial message *can you hear me now* raced incongruously through her mind as she checked for a signal. She didn't have any bars. "Damn," she muttered softly. She'd wanted to be away from civilization, she just hadn't envisioned someone actually disturbing her commune with nature.

"Dax! Dax! You in there?" The loud voice was definitely male. "Turn off that racket, buddy, I can't hear crap out here with the wind."

Vidalia quickly turned down the stereo, her slender frame tense. Was this man someone Dax knew? "W-who are you? And what do you want?" Her voice came out weak and quivery, and she despised the gutless sound of it. Gripping her pepper spray, she forced herself to march to the door and spoke again. "Who are you and what do you want?"

"Dax?"

"No, I'm not Dax," she replied. "But Dax is here, so go away and leave us alone." It was worth a shot if this person was up to no good, but it didn't work.

There was a slight pause and then an amused chuckle. "You must be Vidalia. And if Dax were in there, he would have already been to the door, so give up the lie and open up."

"Who the hell are you," Vidalia challenged, irritation taking over at the sound of the obviously amused male on the other side.

"I'm Dax's neighbor. We could talk a lot better face to face. I can barely hear you over the wind out here."

Vidalia wasn't totally convinced. "Dax never said anything about someone coming over, so why should I believe you? Maybe you just want to rob his place while he's not here. Knowing his name doesn't make you trustworthy in my book."

"If that were so, how would I know your name is Vidalia?" He asked from the other side of the door.

Whoever he might be, he was starting to sound impatient now.

"Dax told me you were coming and asked me to check on you and make sure you got here safely. Since you've got Dax's truck, I thought he might be here after all. There's a big storm brewing, and the electricity could go out any minute. In fact, I'm not even sure I should start back to my own cabin now, it's coming in fast."

Vidalia could indeed see the tree limbs waving ferociously back and forth, some of their leaves brushing against the rails on the deck. If the lights went out, it would be rather eerie up here in the mountains alone. Surely the man was telling the truth, how else would he know her name? Or recognize Dax's truck?

"Come on, Vidalia, open the door," he yelled. "It's starting to rain out here!"

He was right, she could see the water drops slamming against the patio door, their beads of liquid glistening in the glow from the lights as they began to run down the glass panes. If he was a friend of Dax's, she couldn't leave him out there in that storm. Quickly, she unlocked the door and opened it, the wind almost blowing him forward as he ducked inside and slammed it behind him.

She stared at him suspiciously, inspecting the smoky stone color of his eyes and the dark waves of hair that were askew from the wind. He was well over six-foot, rugged jawline, and a sexy light covering of five o'clock shadow on his lower face. His nose had been broken at one time, she decided, noting the small ridge in the cartilage. Dark chocolate brows were an accent to an arresting face, giving him a powerful aura. The rest of his body was dressed in jeans, tan work boots, and a gray sweatshirt, his muscled physique obvious even beneath the loose style clothing. A small sliver of attraction knifed through her.

"Well? Do I pass inspection," he drawled, his lips quirking in amusement.

Embarrassed for acting like an enthralled teenager, Vidalia held up the pepper spray. "If you hadn't, I was prepared. Believe me, I won't hesitate to use it if I have to."

His eyes narrowed at the threat, and for a moment, Vidalia had a weird sense of impending danger. It was gone as suddenly as it came so she thought she must have imagined it. She didn't imagine the next instant though. Suddenly she found herself twisted around in a powerful grip, the pepper spray taken from her fingers, and then quickly released. It had happened so fast it left her mortified at how easily she'd been defeated.

"You...you..." she sputtered. "Give that back!"

He slipped it into the pocket of his pants. "You won't need this while I'm here," he replied. "I'll just keep it for you so you don't get trigger happy unexpectedly," His white teeth flashed in a wicked smile as he took his turn inspecting her.

"Maybe you should go," Vidalia replied acidly, her up-turned nose shooting into the air. She couldn't help the shriek that erupted from her throat when a huge blaze of lightning split the dark sky and thunder boomed so loudly it hurt her ears. "Oh my God!"

The electricity went out and they were instantly pitched into inky darkness, the only light being the flickering firelight casting eerie shadows everywhere. She was trembling so badly she didn't even question the man when he put his arms around her, she just buried her head in his shoulder, whimpering like a small child.

Her mind shifted. Whimpering like *that* small child. The one that haunted her. Dani had been out in weather like this, but there'd been no one to hold her. Only a voice on the phone in the darkness. Her voice.

Vidalia felt her knees giving out on her, and she didn't have the strength to protest when the stranger picked her up and took her to the sofa, easing down onto it with her on his lap. A warm thumb reached out and caressed her cheek, trailing down the coolness of her soft skin.

"Hey, are you okay? You're awfully pale. That was a doozy of a lightning crack, and it sounded pretty close, but we're safe in here." When she didn't answer, he shook her slightly. "Vidalia?"

It took a tremendous effort, but Vidalia willed herself to pull it together. Taking deep breaths, she eased herself off his lap and into a corner of the sofa, pulling her legs up beneath her. With her fists knotted on her knees, she strove to put the lid back on the cannister of emotions the lightning bolt had opened up. It was all right. She was all right. It would be okay. At the back of her mind, she refused to give life to the thought that had raced through her mind every day, every hour of her life since it had happened.

Little Dani Owens would never be okay again—and it was her fault.

"I take it thunderstorms scare you?" He arched a quizzical brow at her, and she forced herself to nod.

"I hate storms."

JAKE STUDIED THE SMALL figure beside him. She looked so miserable and vulnerable that he found himself wishing she was still on his lap. He felt the need to shield and comfort her from the storm and whatever else had driven her into a mountain retreat.

Beyond that, she was a very attractive young woman. His currently dead interest in the opposite sex had flared to life the moment she'd opened the door, her beautiful, deep green eyes staring at him with hostility and mistrust. Dax was forever trying to pair him off with some girl or the other, but none had interested him. They all seemed too immature and spoiled, imagining themselves so tough or talking about bars and men. No, none of them had interested him at all, but this girl was different.

He knew from Dax that Vidalia was an EMS dispatcher, a 911 call taker, and it was a very high stress job. He also knew she'd rejected stress debriefing after a recent incident involving a death. Serving in Afghanistan in a field medical facility, he'd seen people die and been helpless to do anything to save them. Dax had told him very little except that Vidalia hadn't taken the death incident well and had finally requested time off. He'd offered her his cabin and she'd accepted.

For some reason, the American culture didn't face death well as a nation. There was a time when death was a daily part of American life and still was in many nations, but the advent of miracle cures and technology now allowed people to cheat death for longer periods of time than they used to. As a result, death was not all that common for people to have to face until they grew a lot older. And these days it was very common for people to cart their old folks off to nursing homes where they didn't have to watch them die until death was imminent, and even then, they could shield their children from its icy clutches.

"Storms are God's way of cleaning the air," he said quietly. "At least, that's what my mother used to tell me." His eyes twinkled at her, hoping for a small smile. Her slender fingers still shook as they came up to sweep a lock of shining auburn hair behind her delicate ear. "By the way, my name is Jake Bonner. Dax and I are old friends."

She looked at him then, the misery shining in the depths of her eyes. With a deep breath, she offered him a tremulous smile. "I'm Vidalia Minton. I'm sorry for being such a wuss, but I really don't like storms. Plus, I wasn't expecting anyone to be here when I arrived. Dax never said anything about a friend coming by."

"Vidalia, huh? Interesting name, very pretty. I don't think I've ever known anyone named after an onion before," he teased. "I'm sorry if I scared you, but my jeep stalled about half way up your drive, so I walked the rest of the way."

"It's all right," she replied, getting up to put some bigger sticks on the fire that was now burning well. She shivered and put her hands on the backs of her arms. "Just don't call me onion, I got enough of that from my friends when I was a kid."

Jake watched with interest as she bent over to pick up another log to put on the fire. The girl had a very sweet butt and long slender thighs, just the way he liked a nice bottom. "I take it you gave out a few black eyes, then?" He could barely take his eyes off her heart shaped rear, but managed to shift his glance upwards when she turned around.

"Most of my friends call me Vi." She went to the suitcase and laid it on its side to unzip it and take out a sweatshirt. Then she took her flashlight and went into the kitchen area to light the lantern he could see on the counter.

Jake got up and followed her. "I think I prefer Vidalia," he replied. "Beautiful name for a beautiful girl."

Startled, she whirled to face him and he realized she hadn't heard him get up. Her fingers were trembling as she tried to light the wick. Probably more from the cold though, since the temperature was dropping fast and the cabin was barely getting warm.

"Here, let me do that for you," he offered gently, taking the matches from her. "Your hands are freezing. You need to add jeans to that sweatshirt. Or at least some kind of warm pants."

"I'm fine," she said.

A stubborn girl, he decided. He shot her a disapproving look and was amused when her chin lifted in defiance. "Put some pants on, Vidalia," he ordered quietly, unable to help himself. He'd become a commander in his medical unit and people's safety had been a natural concern.

"I said I'm fine," she retorted, although she shifted restlessly from one foot to the other.

Jake clenched his jaw and stared at her. He wasn't used to being disobeyed, and the urge to turn her around and land a few smacks on her shapely little bottom hit him hard. Obviously, he didn't intimidate her, and he supposed that was a good thing, it meant she wasn't afraid of him. On the other hand, a little intimidation wouldn't hurt her, but he chose to back off. "Suit yourself then," he said with a dissatisfied grunt and turned back to his task, ignoring the urge to sit down and pull her over his lap. She wasn't his woman and he had no right.

THE LAST TIME VIDALIA'S heartrate had shot sky high was when she'd run a three-mile race on New Year's Eve with her dispatcher colleagues. It had been so cold outside that her breath had frozen to her muffler when she panted. The race had been for charity for one of the local hospitals in Fort Collins, and she and her friends had been determined to win. And they had, although it hadn't been easy competing against the management team. Dax and his buddies had been good losers though.

She shot Jake a glance out of the corner of her eye as she started putting her supplies into the cabinets. For whatever reason, she was sure he'd wanted to challenge her refusal of help, but hadn't. She felt like challenging him too, and she couldn't explain why. She'd never taken an adversarial role towards a male before, but she found it surprisingly exhilarating.

"There we go," Jake said, turning up the lantern to increase the light.

She pushed her hair back behind her ears with a nervous flutter. "Thank you, that is a lot better. Not as good as electricity, but at least I can see to put things away." She reached into the boxes trying to ignore his intent perusal.

"I'll help you with that," he offered, reaching for one of the boxes on the table.

"No. No, I don't need you to...that is...I can do it myself," she finished lamely, his closeness stealing the air from the immediate proximity. He was having a very odd effect on her.

He ignored her and began taking things out of the box and setting them on the cabinet.

"I said I can do it," she snapped. What in the world was wrong with her? He was only offering to help.

He stopped at the tone in her voice and pinned her in an unblinking stare. "You know, I'm going to start calling you onion if you keep this up."

She flushed and lifted her chin. "I don't need any help—I'm used to doing things on my own."

Jake set the items in his hands down on the table and walked around to her side. "Look," he said grimly, "it seems we're stuck with each other for at least tonight because I'm not going anywhere in this storm. So, I suggest you stop fighting me about every little thing, or you're not going to like the consequences when I get tired of it. And believe me, I'm almost there."

"What do you mean?" Vidalia asked suspiciously, her body tensing. His closeness was affecting her ability to think, and her adrenaline was kicking into overdrive. She found herself wanting to push him and see where it would take her. Trying valiantly to inject some common system back into her overloaded sensory system, she argued with herself. Pushing a stranger beyond his limits could be dangerous. They were up here alone and she didn't know a thing about him except that he was Dax's friend. Something told her that Jake wasn't dangerous, and he wasn't going to hurt her. But what *would* he do?

She studied him through heavy eyelids, gaging her options. There was something else hovering in the air, something she couldn't define. He was glaring at her, his eyes zeroing in on her lips. Would he try to kiss her into submission as they say in the romance novels? She focused on his lips in return and wondered briefly what they would feel like on her own. When he finally stepped towards her and spoke in a determined tone, she was so shocked and surprised she stepped backwards.

"I mean if you keep defying me at every turn, I'm going to put you over my knee and spank you," he said.

Her breath hitched. "You wouldn't!"

"Oh yeah...I would!"

Fear and excitement coursed through Vidalia's body, every nerve ending tingling in disbelief. "But...but...people don't do that in this day and age," she sputtered.

"I do," he replied. "And I'm right on the verge with you."

"You'd damn well better not!"

Jake shook his head with a mocking grin. "You shouldn't have said that, little onion."

Vidalia only had time to wonder how a man as tall as Jake was could move so fast. In a flash he was sitting on one of the kitchen chairs and pulling her down across his long thighs.

"You can't," she yelped, feeling herself falling and unable to do anything about it. She put out her hands to keep herself from hitting the floor, but was surprised to find herself stopped short as his arm wrapped around her waist and held her across his knees.

Vidalia had never been spanked before, but she'd wondered a few times what it might be like whenever she'd come across a scene in a romance novel. It had only been a mild curiosity, though, and not something she felt would ever actually happen. Not in this day and age, and especially not with a complete stranger. The position she was in was mortifying and humiliating as she struggled desperately to get off his lap. She looked back at him in time to see his hand come up in the air. Reality slammed into her psyche and she yelled. "Jake! No!"

"You asked for this," Jake replied grimly, bringing his hand down in a hard, sharp swat on the seat of her jean shorts.

"Ow! Damn!" Vidalia couldn't help the expletive that burst forth from her lips. That smack had hurt. Then it was followed by another and then another. "Ow! Stop it, Jake—that really hurts," she protested.

"Are you going to put on some warm pants?"

He rested his large palm on the seat of her shorts and Vidalia could feel the heat from his hand mingle with the heat of the spanks he'd already administered. When she didn't answer, he lifted his hand and started landing fast hard swats until she kicked and yelled at him again. "Please, just stop."

"Now are you ready to put on some pants?"

"All right, all right," she yelped, "just let me up." Her butt was on fire at this point, and she was ready to agree to the stupid pants if it was that important to him.

"And are you going to be civil and let me help you?"

Vidalia rolled her eyes where he couldn't see them. "Fine...you can help me," she agreed and was rewarded by him picking her up and standing up with her. Her hands immediately flew to the seat of her pants, trying to rub some of the sting out of her butt.

"I'm glad to hear it," Jake replied graciously, his tone mocking as he watched with an amused quirk on his lips. "I'm glad we got that straightened out."

Vidalia ignored him as she took her bag into the bedroom to change into her sweats, and it was then that she realized that for the first time in days she'd actually thought about something else besides Dani Owens.

Trembling, she sat down on the side of the bed, guilt flooding over her once again like a mountain gully washer. What right did she have to be alive when Dani wasn't? Dani had died in a storm much like the one that was raging outside and she hadn't been able to help her. Hadn't been able to get her to safety. It was her job to help save lives and she'd failed one small girl completely. Lost in her misery, she didn't even hear Jake when he called her name.

Chapter 2

"Vidalia?" Jake peered inside the door of the bedroom, wondering what was taking her so long. When he saw her sitting on the side of the bed, her hands lying in her lap and her gaze pinned on the floor, he quickly crossed to her side. "Vidalia? Are you okay?"

When her startled gaze locked with his, Jake was struck by the intense pain that seemed to emanate from her very soul through those luminous green eyes. She shook her head as if she'd been far away from the present and then slowly stood up.

"I'm...I'm fine," she croaked hoarsely, her gaze sliding away. "Really, I'm just fine." She tried to step around him, but he caught her cold hands in his big warm ones.

"Vidalia...if you need to talk, I'm here," he said.

"I don't have anything to talk about, Jake. I'll be fine, really." She pulled her hands from his then and turned around to rummage through her bag for a pair of sweats. She could feel his eyes on her but she didn't want to look at him, didn't want to see the sympathy there. It wasn't deserved.

"Look, Vidalia," he said. "Dax didn't tell me what happened, only that you had refused stress debriefing from an incident in which a death occurred."

Vidalia shot him an angry look. Why did people label life altering events as mere incidents? It was more than an inci-

dent—it was a little girl's life. Couldn't people understand
that? She was the last person to talk to Dani Owens, and no
amount of stress debriefing would change that. Learning to live
with her part in the child's death was the only option left. If she
could. "He didn't have the right to tell you anything," she said
tightly.

His eyes narrowed at her. "You're right, and he didn't give
me any details. But I do have some experience with what you
are going through. It does get easier, but it could get worse if
you don't get some help."

Her words were short and clipped. "I don't need any help,
Jake. I just want to forget it. Forget it ever happened and put
it behind me." God, how she wanted to forget that face that
stayed in her mind. That laughing, smiling face they posted in
the papers haunted Vidalia's every waking moment, and her
sleeping ones too. How she wished she could forget it.

"Did your superiors clear you of fault?" he probed gently.

"Yes, of course," she replied." Now can you leave so I can get
changed?"

Jake hesitated as if he wanted to say more, then sighed.
"Yeah, sure."

When Vidalia returned from the bedroom her face was
pale and closed. It only took a few minutes to get things put
away. "Did you have something in mind for dinner?" he asked
finally, mentally clicking over the things they had put away.
Not much in the way of meat, that was for sure. Except for
some Vienna sausages, canned chicken, deli meats, and cheese
hot dogs. No real man food like steaks, brats, or chops. Oh, and
plenty of baked goods and treats. The girl must love her chocolate. Then again, he hadn't met a woman yet that didn't.

Vidalia shrugged. "Not really, I don't cook much. Usually, I just have some soup or something," she waved her hand vaguely as if dinner would forever remain a mystery in her life.

Jake chuckled. "The life of a dispatcher who is always on call, and always changing shifts. I get it."

"There is that," she agreed with a quick grin. "I was working second shift when I took vacation, so dinner at everyone else's dinnertime is a distant memory."

Her face was getting some color back and she seemed a bit more relaxed to Jake. "How about some grilled cheese?" he asked.

Her eyebrow arched. "And how would we do that exactly? Last time I checked, there was no electricity."

Good grief, that was almost a glacier thaw. Apparently, the girl could show some snark. Jake went to the laundry room off the kitchen and came back carrying a green camp stove that looked to have seen better days. He grinned in victory. "Me and Dax always keep one of these beauties on hand for just such an occasion," he said proudly as he sat it on the gleaming stovetop.

Vidalia couldn't help smiling. The triumph in his eyes might have been equivalent to going out and hunting his own dinner and bringing it home to the little woman. "Do you have the propane to go with it?"

"Of course," he said. He ducked back into the laundry room and came out carrying two different bottles of it. "Right here." He held them up with relish.

"Well, then, I'm game for some grilled ham and cheese if you're cooking. Unless you're one of those antiques who think a woman's place is barefoot and pregnant in the kitchen," she barbed delicately.

He laughed out loud. "I'm a believer in all things being up for discussion and doing what each person likes and does best. I don't mind cooking, it's not my favorite hobby, but I don't mind it." He gave her the side eye. "I take it you don't like cooking?"

"Actually, I enjoy cooking when I have time to do it. I especially enjoy baking." She reached in to the cabinet over the sink and took one of the Rubbermaid containers she'd stored up there. "I especially like to make these," she said. After taking the lid off she dipped her hand in and came out with one of the biggest cookies Jake had ever seen and took a huge bite out of it.

"What is that?" He asked, reaching over and taking it from her hand. Her cheeks were bugling with the delightful looking treat.

"Mumm," she mumbled.

Jake eyed the monstrous cookie and identified chocolate chips, M&Ms, raisins, and coconut right off the bat. Throwing caution to the winds, he took a big bite. The explosion of flavor was sweet, chocolatey, and heavenly.

Her eyes were laughing at him as she reached over and took her cookie back. Once she'd swallowed, she enlightened him. "It's a monster cookie—has about everything you can think of in it. A great way to get rid of almost empty bags of stuff that you can't use for anything else. Don't pitch it—make a cookie.

"That is a great cookie," he said reverently, bending down and taking another bite from the cookie in her fingers. "Ith tha a moshmalo?"

"What?" Vidalia asked as she took the last bite.

Jake swallowed. "I said, is that a marshmallow? I thought I tasted marshmallow."

She nodded, chewing down the last morsel. "Yes, mini-marshmallows."

He stared at her mouth, itching to kiss that bit of chocolate off her lips. Watching her enjoy the treat did funny things to him. His buddy down below was getting restless. He mentally groaned when she swiped the chocolate off with her pink tongue. When her eyes darkened and she backed up slightly, he mentally shook himself and turned away. "Now for that grilled ham and cheese."

"I-I'll get the stuff from the fridge," she said breathlessly.

Jake heard her put the cookie container lid on and set it on the counter. When she moved out of his proximity, he sighed in relief and bent to concentrate on getting the camp stove functioning.

They finally sat down to grilled ham and cheese sandwiches and tomato soup, all compliments of the camp stove. Dax kept the kitchen stocked with dishes and cooking equipment, so no problem there. A guarded camaraderie had developed and it was rather cozy to be sitting in the warming cabin while the rain kept up a steady tattoo against the French windows on the patio deck. It was totally black outside but the lanterns Dax kept on hand, plus the fireplace, cast a comforting glow over the room.

"So, how long do you plan on staying here?" Jake asked softly as they were finishing dinner.

"I've got the cabin for the next two weeks, if I want it that long," she replied. "I'm just taking it one day at a time."

"Do you mind if I visit you?"

Vidalia shrugged her slender shoulders. "I guess you can come over now and then. I really don't care."

Jake winced. "Ouch...that hurt."

"You asked," she replied. Her eyes were huge in the fire-light—and very wary.

Jake made a mental note to call Dax tomorrow when he went to get his jeep. If it wouldn't start, he'd have to haul it back to his cabin where he could work on it. But first of all, he wanted to know exactly what had happened to Vidalia Minton. It was obvious he wasn't going to get any information from her.

AFTER CLEANING UP DINNER remains, they moved to the couch and each sat in their respective corners sipping hot chocolate and staring at the fire. The silence wasn't actually awkward, it was almost peaceful. Vidalia enjoyed the warm glow and the dim lighting; it hid a lot of emotions she'd rather not deal with. She didn't mind talking about her family or other common subjects, but she drew the line at her job. That was a minefield she staunchly stayed away from.

"So how do you know Dax?" She finally asked.

"We went to the same high school in Denver," he explained. "After that I joined the service for eight years and then bought the property my cabin sits on. The adjoining property belongs to my parents. It's close enough to the main road that I've spent most of my time there this last year or so."

"What about in the middle of winter when the pass is closed?" she asked.

"I'm staying with my parents in Denver until I decide where I want to buy a house," he explained. "Right now, I'm not sure what I want to do yet, so I'm taking some time off."

"What did you do in the service?" Vidalia was really curious now. At dinner he'd been peppering her with questions and saying nothing about himself. He hesitated briefly and a shadow crossed his face. It occurred to Vidalia that maybe Jake was doing some hiding of his own. His reply was tight.

"I worked in the medical tents," he said frankly. "I'm not going to lie—it was pretty rough. I was an EMT before I went in so that's where they put me when I signed up. When I wasn't on call, I was studying medical training online."

"It's interesting that you and Dax both ended up in the medical field," she mused, watching the fire sending dancing shadows about the room.

"Well, I can't say it's really a medical field. More like emergency training, I guess. Although, I was planning on going to med school when I returned. But I'm not solid with that yet." He got up and put some more logs on the fire.

Vidalia watched his smooth, fluid movements, the muscles tensing in his strong thighs when he crouched down. Attraction stirred restlessly once again in her abdomen. When he returned to the couch, she was hyper aware of him. Her skin prickled when he sat down closer to her than his corner. She glanced down at her watch. "It's almost 9:30 pm no wonder I'm tired. I think I'll just go to bed." She knew she wouldn't be able to sleep, but sitting here with Jake so close wasn't an option either. She could feel his interest. At any other time, she'd be interested right back, but not right now.

"You might want to sleep here on the couch tonight, since the electricity is still out," Jake replied with a nod.

"Where will you sleep then?" She stood up and gazed down at him.

"I'll sleep in the loft. Heat rises and there aren't any doors to close except for the bathroom."

"I'll just sleep in the bedroom and leave the door ajar," she decided. "That way some of the heat will get in there. You can have the couch and keep the fire going."

His eyebrow arched. "You're a bossy little thing, aren't you?"

"You invited yourself over," she reminded him with a grin. "The least you can do is keep wood on the fire."

He stood up and towered over her with a gleam in his eye. "I can think of few other fires I'd like to start."

Vidalia blushed and quickly headed for her bedroom. Her heart rate had picked up and she was half afraid he might follow her.

"Coward," he taunted softly.

"Bully," she retorted, glancing over her shoulder just as she slipped inside. Against his advice, she closed the door and locked it. How could she sleep without fear with that testosterone overload sleeping on her couch?

"Leave the door ajar, Vidalia," he ordered through the wooden barrier.

"Go away," she replied haughtily.

"I won't bother you, I promise. Although, you need a good spanking in my opinion. I can guarantee you'd sleep well afterwards."

"I don't care about your opinion," she retorted.

"You've certainly made that clear."

She hesitated. "Can I really trust you to keep your word, Jake?"

"Vidalia, you can trust me. I won't cross this threshold unless you want me to," he mocked.

"That's not going to happen, but I'll take your word for it." She unlocked the door and stepped back, leaving it ajar.

"Good girl," he said softly, his eyes traveling up and down her slender frame. It felt like he was touching her because everywhere his gaze trailed seemed to light on fire.

Her voice came out in a whisper. "Just make sure you don't come in."

The last thing Vidalia needed was a man in her life. It was complicated enough right now and she couldn't handle the emotion it would take to be vested in a relationship. She felt brittle all the time, like she would shatter into a million pieces if someone hurt her.

"Sleep well," he replied, turning away and leaving her in peace.

Vidalia heaved a sigh of relief. Jake was really a charming man and she liked everything about him so far except for this spanking thing. In fact, she was so aware of him that it scared her and she regretted challenging him. It had brought them to a level of closeness now that she wished she didn't have with him.

She didn't want anyone getting close.

Another heartache was the last thing she needed. All she wanted was to be left alone to figure out how to handle this huge load that was weighing her down. Until she could figure that out, she had nothing left to offer to anyone else but a broken shell of herself.

Quickly she changed into her pajamas and crawled into bed with a flashlight and book to keep her mind from concentrating on the trauma that had driven her into the mountains. Her heart ached for Dani Owens, and she knew that little girl had changed her life. Nothing would ever be the same. Her brain told her there had been nothing more she could have done, but her heart told her differently. She couldn't seem to get past it, and her restless mind was always going back and replaying the conversation in her mind, searching for answers, trying to figure out how she could have done it better.

After three hours of reading, dozing, and waking up in a cold sweat, she finally gave in and took a sleeping tablet. It was the only way she ever got any real rest. The doctor had given them to her for emergencies. They would be gone soon though, but she didn't feel any closer to getting relief than she had previously.

She briefly thought of Jake in the living room on the couch. She supposed he would be comfortable, but if not, oh well. He'd invited himself to stay over, so it wasn't any concern of hers whether or not the couch was comfortable. With any luck he would be gone before she got up.

Snuggled under the covers, Vidalia waited for blessed sleep. At least, she would get a few hours rest before her dreams starting coming alive. It seemed they never left her alone anymore, and it was getting worse.

Light was barely breaking through her window when Vidalia woke up with a start. Her chest was heaving, and her forehead damp with perspiration. She looked wildly around the room trying to recognize where she was. Instant memory suddenly served her, and she realized she was at Dax's cabin—and she had been dreaming again. Weird dreams.

Lightning bolts had been chasing her. Lightning bolts with faces. They'd been laughing at her and trying to stab her with their energy jolts. Beyond them was a still figure, a small girl with blond hair lying on the ground. Vidalia couldn't get to her. She wanted to get to her, but how? The lightning bolts were surrounding her. They were stinging her, and she couldn't move.

With a heavy yawn, Vidalia sat up in bed and glanced at her watch. It was 5:00 am and she had gotten a little over four hours sleep according to her Fitbit. She felt incredibly tired. She pushed her hair out of her face, tucked the damp strands along her forehead behind her ears, and swung her feet to the floor. No point in going back to sleep, this was as good as it got. Maybe she could get a nap later on, but for now, she wanted to get up and away from the dreams.

Quickly she dressed in sweats and running shoes and padded into the kitchen to make coffee. She would have some coffee on the veranda and go for a walk as the sun was coming up, then come back and eat breakfast.

Coming into the living room, Vidalia stopped short as she realized that Jake was still asleep on the couch. She'd forgotten about him. Deciding she didn't want to wake him making coffee, she slipped out the front door instead.

Once outside, she breathed deeply of the clean mountain air and looked around her with interest. The darkness wasn't quite so dark since the sun was trying to wake up. Everything looked wet from the storm last night and there were leaves strewn across the deck as if a giant had slapped the trees and knocked bits out of them. She started down the gravel drive that went back out to the main road figuring she would walk back and forth a couple of times for some exercise, then do some hiking later. Dax had said there were several trails around and had given her a map.

It really did feel good to be away from the hustle and bustle of the city. Vidalia enjoyed her walk and the rising of the sun in all its glory. It brought light and warmth to a new day. She stopped to watch a couple of chipmunks chasing each other around a tree trunk, and smiled at their antics.

When she came upon Jakes jeep, she was delighted to see a squirrel getting a drink out of the puddle on the soft top as she approached. Peering inside, she noted that it was fairly clean, no drink cups rolling around in the floorboard. She couldn't say that was always the case with her little Ford Focus.

Moving on, her step was lighter and her spirits rose. It had been a while since she'd done anything like this, and she was grateful that Dax had made the offer.

As she rounded the corner of the cabin on her third time back, she saw Jake sitting at the wooden table on the deck, a pot of coffee and two mugs sitting in front of him. He smiled at her, and Vidalia's breath caught in her throat. How could a man look so sexy first thing in the morning?

"GOOD MORNING! COME on up and have some coffee," Jake invited with a lazy smile. I have to assume you drink it since you brought it with you."

Vidalia nodded and took the other chair while he poured her a cup of the hot steaming brew. It smelled heavenly and the cup warmed her hands.

"Cream and sugar?"

She nodded again, and he poured a bit of the creamer she'd brought and took a sugar cube out of the box.

"One or two lumps?"

"One," she replied.

"She speaks!" He exclaimed, his eyes twinkling at her. "I was beginning to think you were just going to point and nod."

Vidalia couldn't help but chuckle, he was infectious. "It seems you're in a chipper mood this morning. Are you this way every morning?"

"Only when I'm with a beautiful woman," he replied.

Vidalia felt a flush creep up her throat. She didn't feel beautiful at all, she'd just got out of bed. What she felt like was a dragged-out hag, but it was sweet of him to say so.

They chatted amiably, Jake carefully avoiding the land mine of her job. One never realizes how much their job is a part of their life until they try to avoid talking about it, but he managed.

"Would you like a granola bar," Vidalia finally asked, her stomach beginning to growl. "Or some strawberries? I brought up some fresh ones yesterday." She stood up to go get the proffered goodies.

Jake stood up too. "What? No bacon and eggs? Or sausage and biscuits? What kind of a cook are you?" His eyebrows waggled in mock protest.

"The kind that doesn't have time to cook," she responded dryly, "I'm always on call. Remember?"

"Yes, I know what you mean," Jake said softly as he watched the smile fade from her face. They had stepped on the land mine. When she came back with breakfast, the conversation was somewhat stilted, and they both made a conscious effort not to go there. "So, what are your plans for today?" he finally asked.

Vi seemed to brighten at the question. "I'm planning on doing some hiking. My parents always wanted to buy a cabin but could never afford it," she said wistfully. "This is a real treat for me."

"Have you hiked a lot? I know that seems like a dumb question since you're from Fort Collins," he added. "But hiking in bear country can be different."

Her eyes widened. "Have you seen a lot of bears up here?"

"A few," he admitted. The population of black bears has grown a lot in the last 40 years. No grizzlies though, they are mostly up towards the Canadian and Alaskan borders. A few in Idaho maybe."

"I'm aware of the campground rules in the Rocky Mountain National Park and other tent camping areas, but overall, there have been very few bear attacks. All the information I've read say they stay away from humans. Since this is a developed area here in Skokie Pass, and mostly cabins, I'd assumed I wouldn't need any bells or sprays," she added. "Besides, I haven't always lived in Fort Collins. My parents moved there from Missouri three years ago. So, no, I've not been in this area all my life."

Jake nodded. "Well, it is spring here. Most of the bear populations are about 7000 to 10,000 feet. We are about 4500 feet here, I checked when I bought my cabin," he said. "Spring is when they start to come out of hibernation and are more active. Also, very hungry. And sometimes the females will have a cub they are extremely protective of."

"Anything special I should be aware of?" Vidalia asked with a frown.

"Don't put trash out at night," he replied. "If you are going to put it outside, make sure you put it out in the morning, or take it to a dumping station as quickly as possible. Bears can smell food a mile away."

Vidalia was looking extremely nervous. "What if I see one while I'm hiking? Am I supposed to lay flat on the ground and let it sniff me?"

Jake laughed. "No, that's with a grizzly bear. With a black bear, don't run or try to climb a tree. They are really good climbers, and they can run at 35 miles per hour, so you'll never outrun them. Just stand still and hold your arms out, or above your head. Whatever you can do to appear larger. If they stand on their hind legs, they are trying to see you better, so don't be tempted to run. They are very curious at times, but really do shy away from people. The chance of you encountering one is slim to none, but if you do, and it's aggressive, then fight. If you have bear spray, spray the eyes and then run. They'll most likely take off in the opposite direction."

"What are the chances of surviving an attack?" Vidalia asked, her eyes wide.

"Really good, actually. They don't like loud noise, like bells or whistles. You can throw your backpack at them, which is a good reason to wear one. They are curious, and if they smell food in it, they will turn their attention to the pack while you leave the area," he said. "If you have a hiking stick, use that if they are attacking you, and yell like a crazy woman."

Vidalia glanced uneasily at the forest surrounding them and Jake took pity on her. "Don't worry, you are very unlikely to run into one. I just wanted you to be aware and know what to do if you did. Do you have any bear spray?"

"No. It never occurred to me that I would need it."

"Just make noise as you hike then," he replied. "They shy away from humans, and if they know you're coming, you'll never see them."

She looked relieved then. "We always make noise when hiking in Missouri too," she said. "More because of snakes though. You don't want to come up on any rattlesnakes unannounced. Plus, there can be bobcats around, although I don't know anyone who has ever seen one. But they say they are there."

"Why did your parents move out here?" Jake asked curiously. "That's quite a life-style change."

"My dad got a job offer in Fort Collins. Plus, my mom has a sister that lives out here. Since my grandparents have been gone, she kind of wanted to get closer to her. She doesn't have any other brothers or sisters."

"I take it you have no siblings?"

She shook her head. "No, I'm an only child. So, they have no grandchildren yet either."

Jake studied her. "What about you? Are you happy with the move?"

Vidalia shrugged. "I was just out of high school and not sure where I wanted to go to college. I was looking at a community college, but not sure what I wanted to take. Plus, I've always been fascinated with the mountains. We used to go to the Ozarks a lot, but it was still pretty warm and humid to hike there. When they said they were moving and wanted me to come with them, I agreed."

Jake was pleased that Vidalia seemed to be talking a little more. All he'd gotten out of her last night was the kind of music she liked, a few movies she'd watched, and tons of silence while watching the fire flicker.

She was starting to appear restless so not wanting to push his luck he stood up and stretched. "Well, I need to go see about my jeep since my cell phone doesn't work back in here."

"Yes, I know, mine didn't have any service either," she agreed, standing up too.

"I guess I'll walk out to the road and make a few calls." He'd started toward the steps when Vidalia made an offer.

Chapter 3

"Why don't you take Dax's truck? That way if you need to run into town for parts or something, you'll have a way to get there."

Jake turned around, a smile lighting up his face. "That would be great, Vidalia. I really appreciate the offer.

He hesitated then spoke again. "Would you like to come with me?"

Vidalia shook her head. "No, not today. I want to get settled in and explore the area a little bit. Maybe I'll go another time." She got up to get the keys to the truck.

Slightly disappointed, Jake followed her into the cabin. "All right. But how about I fix steaks on the grill tonight in payment for using the truck?" He waited for her to turn him down again.

When she let her guard down, he was reasonably sure she found him attractive, just as he did her. It might take some work to get through her defenses though. She seemed determined to shut everyone out and wallow in her self-conceived failure of losing someone on her watch. It was the last thing she needed to do, and he knew that from personal experience.

Vidalia handed him the keys. "I usually just have a sandwich after work..." Her voice trailed off, and she shot him a glance. Probably hoping he would take the hint, but he had no intention of doing so.

"You're not at work now, you're on vacation," he replied firmly. "And I intend to help you have a good time." His voice was full of promise and then he put his arms around her and gave her a friendly hug. A delicate pink tinged her cheeks and her breath quickened at his closeness. Jake knew he'd been right about her attraction to him. "See you tonight."

Before she could refuse, he took the keys and headed out the door, pausing to wave after he turned the black pickup around and headed down the drive. She'd followed him outside and was staring after him with her arms folded across her middle, her face unreadable. She did wave back though.

JAKE PARKED AT THE end of the gravel lane and flipped open his cell phone to make a call to Dax.

"Dax Manning, here," came the disembodied voice in the phone.

"Hi Dax. It's Jake."

"Hey, Jake. Did Vi make it up there?"

"Yes, she did, but she's petrified of storms. There was a big one up here last night," Jake replied, watching a rabbit leaping across the road.

"That's understandable."

"Yeah, the electricity went out so I stayed over last night."

"You stayed over?" Dax echoed. "She let you stay over?"

"Technically, I didn't give her much choice," Jake said. "My jeep broke down on the way over here and it was starting to pour down rain once I arrived. I had no intention of walking three miles home in all that lightning and wind. It was blowing branches off trees."

"Well, did you two have a good time?" Dax asked curiously.

"Hardly. Getting her to talk was like pulling hen's teeth. Non-existent."

Dax laughed. "Vi's a pretty private person."

There was silence for a few seconds, then Jake said, "Dax, what happened that Vi won't talk about? I can tell it's really bothering her."

Jake could hear the sigh on the other end of the line. "You've seen the news about the ten-year-old girl they found in the ravine up in Rangers Pass?"

"The one that was killed in the flash flood several weeks ago?"

"Yeah...that's the one," Dax replied. "Her name was Dani Owens."

"I do remember something about it in the paper. She got separated from her parents or something like that, and called 911 in the middle of a thunderstorm?" Jake tried to remember the article, but couldn't recall all the details."

"That's the one," Dax said. "Vi got the call that night. She couldn't get the girl to do any of the things she asked her to because she was so terrified. She'd told VI she was in Rangers Pass, but the phone went dead in the middle of the call. By the time the medics found her, a flash flood had ravaged the ravine, and they found Dani's body near the bottom. Vi blames herself. She thinks she should have been able to talk Dani into getting out of the ravine or getting above the water, but the little girl was too petrified to move."

"What a hard call for Vi," Jake murmured sympathetically. "There's only so much a person can do for someone else, and Vi has to face that fact sooner or later."

"We thought she was okay with it since she refused stress debriefing. But she's been getting short tempered and super tired at work, which means she isn't sleeping well. We could all tell she was still stressed out about it. Ross suggested she take some time off and she said she'd been going to ask that very thing. He was relieved because he didn't want to order her into stress debrief if she didn't want to. So, I offered her my four-wheel drive and the keys to the cabin."

"Taking time off was smart of her," Jake agreed.

"Vi is damned good at her job, one of the best dispatchers we have," Dax replied. "I hope she's able to make the transition, or I'm afraid she'll end up quitting or losing her job. I'd hate to see either of those things happen."

"Yeah, I can see that," Jake replied. "Dealing with loss-related stress can be extremely difficult, especially if you bottle it all up inside."

"If anyone can understand, it's you, buddy," Dax replied quietly. "Maybe it's a good thing you two met."

"I don't know if she thinks so," Jake replied, thinking of the spanking he'd given Vidalia the night before. "She's really stubborn, and you know me...I don't do stubborn females."

Dax chuckled. "Don't tell me you..."

"I did," Jake interrupted him. He told Dax what had happened the night before.

"It must just be your winning personality," Dax teased. "Vi has always been cooperative here at work. The epitome of good behavior."

"She wasn't last night," Jake growled.

"Well, maybe you can get through to her. If you can, I'd sure appreciate it. She's a good friend, and I hate to see her hurting like this."

"Is that all she is?" Jake was surprised at himself, the flare of jealousy strong as the question popped from his lips.

"Uh...yeah...that's all for me. Why? Don't tell me you're finally interested in a woman," Dax crowed. "You are! I'll be damned—it couldn't happen to a nicer couple."

"Hey, don't go marrying us yet," Jake protested with a laugh. "I've got to get her to talk to me first."

"Well—good luck, buddy. Let me know how it turns out. I'll be waiting with bated breath."

"You're a clown," Jake said, hanging up. It was time to get on with his jeep and do a little shopping. The evening awaited and so did Vidalia. At least for tonight. He'd practically had to strongarm her into dinner. He wondered if she had actually mourned for Dani yet? Or cried?

VIDALIA WATCHED AS the pickup disappeared down the lane, some of her tenseness dissipating. Taking a few deep cleansing breaths, she decided to look around the cabin area.

It was the beginning of spring, the time when mother nature once more wrapped her cloak around her with new buds and leaves on the trees. Early colorful flowers nestled among the blossoming shrubbery, peeking their heads out for the rain and the warming sunshine.

The cabin was built on a fairly flat area, but still on a mild slope, which fell away more sharply in the back. Through the trees, she could see what looked like a meadow or a clearing down below, perhaps about 200 yards away. She was sure there was a stream down there somewhere and wanted to be able to take some photos of the water and the rocks. There was always a mountain stream when you were up in the Rockies, the snow melt insured that. Cold and refreshing, but certainly not something you'd want to swim in.

Excited at the prospect; she hurried inside to get a shower and change. The electricity was back on, it had flipped on while they sat on the deck. Kudos to the work crews who'd found whatever problem had caused it to go off.

Cell phone...check. First aid kit...check. Area map...check. Money...check.

Dressed in appropriate hiking boots, jeans, and a long-sleeved t-shirt, Vidalia set off down the worn path towards the meadows. After Jake's earlier warnings about bears, she decided to stick to trails already worn by human feet. The light pack she had on her back held a couple of bottles of water and a few cracker snacks. Nothing meaty that might attract bears, she'd decided. Keeping an eye out for a walking stick, she finally spied one that looked sturdy and was about shoulder high. Her pocketknife took care of the twigs and leaves attached. She swished it through the air a few times to make sure she could handle it.

She didn't know if she'd pick up cell service or not, but it was worth a shot in case she moved into range. And the cash was to get lunch at Smokie's Diner near the trailhead to Victory Falls, which she would run into when she turned back west towards the main road. Dax said it was really good food.

The path Vidalia was on took her through the meadow and into the woods on the south side. There she found a connection to the hiking trail for the falls that Dax had told her about. To her right was about a half-mile hike up to the falls and to her left was the half-mile back to the main road. So, a nice little hike for her first morning in the woods since she was planning on going both ways.

The Victory waterfall was amazing. Vidalia spent a long time photographing it from different angles. Two long waterfalls fell at enough of an angle down through the rocks that the splash of the falls at the bottom formed a V. The view from the long wooden bridge in front of the pool and subsequent stream was the best angle for shots.

Up near the base of the falls was a sandy area on the left side that Vidalia would like to get to, but she couldn't see any paths through the dense pines and shrubs to indicate anyone had gone over there. She was just considering ignoring Jake's advice to stick to the manmade trails when she saw movement in the shrubbery near the sand base. She gasped when she saw a small black cub dart out of the bushes and run to the water's edge.

Oh my god! There were bears here. Her heart beating fast, she watched as the mother stepped out behind her cub. Ducking down she took her camera out and set it between the rails of the bridge and started taking pics. She froze when she heard the sound of childish laughter behind her.

Glancing down the trail to her right, Vidalia saw a young girl and what must be an older brother holding her hand, coming up the trail. She held her palm out towards them and then put her finger to her lips. She made a ducking motion with her hand and they responded by ducking down. "Bears," she mouthed, and pointed through the railing towards the falls.

Looking down at the bears, she saw the mother entering the water with her cub and drinking deeply from the stream. The two kids behind her inched forward and nestled in behind her.

"Wow," whispered the little girl. "This is so cool."

"Where are your parents?" Vidalia whispered.

"They're slow," the older teen responded.

They all watched the bears in fascination as the bears actually played in the water, the sunshine glistening off their blackish pelts. Vidalia took a ton of pics, and so did the kids.

"Marion!" The call came from the path down and they all swiveled to see a couple coming up the path, the woman in front obviously red-faced and irritated. The man behind her hollered again. "Marion, the kids are fine, they just went ahead. In fact, there they are now," he said loudly as he pointed towards Vidalia and the children.

Vidalia glanced back through the railing. The mother bear was standing at attention, sniffing the air. She kept taking pictures until the bear suddenly whirled around and pushed her baby ahead of her to disappear into the brush. Jake was right again, Vidalia decided. They were very shy.

The two kids jumped up and started yelling at their parents for scaring off the bears. Their mother turned as white as a sheet and the father was silent with shock. "Bears?" he finally squeaked.

The children were excitedly showing their parents their cell phone photos as Vidalia slipped away and headed back down the path.

"Oh my god," the father exclaimed, "she has a cub. Come on, kids, we need to leave this area immediately."

Vidalia agreed, her knees still trembling. As exciting as it had been to spot the bears, it was also frightening.

It was a mile back to the main road, and then Vidalia stepped out of the woods at the trailhead for Victory Falls. Across the road was the diner. It was 11:45 am. Perfect timing for lunch.

Or at least a diet coke.

She hadn't had much appetite for days now but the smell of burgers in the air did smell good when she stepped inside and went up to the deli counter.

"Where did you come from?" asked the perky, short-haired brunette behind the counter. Her curious blue eyes gave Vidalia the once-over. "I didn't hear a car pull up."

"I just came down the trailhead for Victory Falls," Vidalia replied. "Those cheeseburgers smell really heavenly. Could I get one of those?"

"They are the best," she enthused. "Cheeseburger, Joe," she called over her shoulder to the cook behind the gleaming steam table. He grunted and the meat sizzled when he threw it on the hot grill.

"Are you staying in one of the cabins?" the young girl asked curiously.

Vidalia nodded, inhaling the mouthwatering aroma. "Yes, Dax Manning's cabin."

"Oh, yeah, I know Dax." The girl snapped her fingers suddenly. "I knew you looked familiar. You're that 911 dispatcher from the paper. The one that got Dani Owen's call. Wow, that was a hard call. I'm so sorry."

And just like that, Vidalia's appetite disappeared. "Uh, never mind," she said tightly. "I'm not hungry after all." She turned around and headed for the door.

"Hey, wait. I'm sorry," the girl called after her.

Vidalia didn't even hear her. In that single instant, it all came crashing down on her again. Of course, there had been an inquiry. Accusations. Horrible references to irresponsible dispatchers in the past. When tragedy strikes, the masses call for blood, someone to take the blame. Anyone but them.

Somehow her picture had been leaked to the papers and then retracted, but the damage had been done. It had all finally died down once the inquiry was over. No one had blamed her in the end, but Vidalia had never stopped blaming herself.

Occasionally, like today, someone would recognize her and the pain would cut deep all over again. Even though she'd changed her hairstyle and wore sunglasses when she went out, she'd still been recognized now and then. Quickly, she sprinted across the road, back up the path that cut along the meadow below her cabin, and then finally back up the hill to her sanctuary.

Inside the bedroom she grabbed the bottle of sleeping tablets and took one. Then she sank down on the bed, her hands over her ears in a useless effort to block out Dani's terrified cries.

JAKE STOPPED AT SMOKIE'S Diner about 2:00 pm to grab some beer before heading to his cabin for a shower. His jeep hadn't taken long to repair, and he'd used the pickup to haul it back to Dax's cabin, and then done his grocery shopping. Vidalia hadn't been there when he'd parked the pickup in its spot in the driveway, so he'd assumed she was still out hiking.

"Hey, Poke, how you doing?" he asked the bubbly brunette. Her face didn't look bubbly today though. "Everything okay? Did your boyfriend cancel your date tonight?" he teased, trying to brighten her mood.

"Ha ha—funny man," she replied, flicking her bar towel at him. "I'm fine, but I did something stupid a few hours ago that I regret."

Her eyes were almost teary and Jake was surprised. "What did you do, kiddo?"

"There was a woman who came in and ordered a cheeseburger around noon and I knew she looked familiar. I finally placed her. It was that woman who took the 911 call about that little girl who died in Rangers Pass," she replied sadly. "When I recognized her, she canceled her cheeseburger and ran out of here like a ghost was chasing her. I tried to stop her. I said I was sorry, but she just flew across the road and into Victory Falls trailhead. I hope she's okay." She bit her lip, staring up at Jake with huge eyes.

Jake's eyes narrowed. "It wasn't your fault, Poke, she's pretty sensitive about that case."

"Do you know her?" Poke asked.

"I know she's staying at Dax's cabin," Jake said. "I met her last night when Dax asked me to check on his friend and make sure she got there safely. I don't really know her though."

"I wish she'd let me apologize," Poke said wistfully. "Sometimes I just don't think before my mouth opens.

"A trait totally common to women," he teased.

"Oh, you!" Poke threw her towel at him, but a grin stole across her face. "We girls aren't the only ones capable of sticking our feet in our mouths."

"Don't worry about it, Poke," Jake said kindly. "I'm going by there to check on her again, so I'll pass along your heartfelt apology. She seems like a really nice person and you probably just caught her off guard."

"Thanks, Jake," Poke replied, taking his cash payment. "And tell her she has a cheeseburger coming on me anytime she wants it. I had a cousin who was a dispatcher and she said it's a job that will tear your heart out. It takes an amazing person to stay in a job like that for very long. They are the unsung heroes behind the scenes that never get much credit for the work they do."

"I'll tell her, Poke," Jake agreed as he took his change and grabbed the case of beer. She was right, he reflected. If a battle was won on the battlefield, the generals got the credit. The medical teams got the leftovers, the damaged and the wounded. The ones whose lives would never be the same. If the medical team was able to save a life so that the soldier could receive a purple heart, no one ever knew the name of the medic who stopped that arterial bleed, or who stood by their patient until the crises point was past.

In police work, the cops with the takedowns get all the credit. And their superiors above them. The dispatchers behind the scenes, the ones who take the desperate calls of those who need help, are the support team. Rarely noticed, barely thanked, they keep everything running smoothly, hand out names and addresses, tell the cops where to go, run all the checks on the bad guy behind the scenes, and report back to the officers every bit of information gleaned at their fingertips. How many dispatchers stand beside the officer who receives recognition for saving a life?

Children were the hardest loss of all, as he well knew. He reflected on his own experience. Young children used as shields in their parents' war were a heartbreaking loss. He'd grown quite fond of Hamal. He'd been brought in when his parents had been killed and lost a huge amount of blood. Jake had taken over his care personally. Saving Hamal the first time had been easy. Saving him the second time had been impossible. Jake had taken it hard and blamed himself for the longest time.

Finally focusing on the road to his cabin, Jake put thoughts of Hamal out of his mind. It was hard to close that door sometimes, but it got easier with the passage of time. It was time to focus on Vidalia Minton.

Jake was attracted to the gorgeous girl on many levels. She raised his protective instincts, he was in love with her heart-shaped ass, and her sassy mouth was meant to be kissed by him. Helping her right now was his most important mission. Starting with dinner tonight.

Chapter 4

"Jake, I don't know when I've enjoyed a steak quite so much," Vidalia said, patting her stomach. She hadn't eaten a thing all day except for the granola bar on her hike and a bottle of water. The fiasco at Smokie's had thrown her for a loop, but the nap had helped a lot. The sleeping pill had given her about three hours this afternoon, without wild dreams waking her up. She was still pondering on that. Was it the exercise that had helped?

When Jake had come over around 5:00 pm she'd even been excited to see him. He'd grilled those T-bones to perfection while she prepared the salad laced with Gouda cheese. Something about the mountain air had seemed to increase her appetite.

Jake cocked his head to the side and grinned at her. "You mean you actually ate more than half a dozen bites? Cause it hardly looks like you've eaten."

"I'm not a big eater," she protested with a laugh.

"You're going to have to eat more than that, or you're going to start losing weight."

"I will—I'm just not that hungry lately," she replied defensively getting up to clear their plates away. "Like I said, I've never been a big eater." She didn't tell him she'd already lost nine pounds over the last six weeks. "I can't stand dishes in the sink," she added. "I'd rather do them now and get it out of the way. Once the food dries on them they are harder to clean." She began gathering dishes.

Jake nodded assent and stood up to help her. "So, I have a message for you from Poke," he said, grabbing condiments to stuff in the fridge.

"Who is Poke?" she asked.

"I call her Poke, but her name is actually Pauline," Jake replied. "She works at Smokie's Diner."

Vidalia stiffened and shot him a side eye. "What message?"

"She said to tell you that you have a free burger on her anytime you want it, and that she's really sorry she upset you. She actually admires you and the work that dispatchers do."

"That was nice of her," Vidalia said. She started rinsing dishes and putting them into the dishwasher. When Jake's hand touched her chin, she started.

"She really is sorry, Vidalia," he said gently, turning her face up to his. "You should stop by and see her."

"That's not a conversation I want to revisit." Vidalia stepped away from him and went back to the table. She could feel Jake studying her while she worked.

"You need to talk about it," he insisted.

Vidalia flung her hands in the air and scowled at him. "Not with every Tom, Dick, and Harry who wants to gossip." The evening had been pleasant so far, the food preparations keeping them busy with little reason to talk much, but now that dinner was over, Vidalia was becoming increasingly nervous. Especially with the current conversation.

Jake sighed with frustration. "Will you just go back to the diner while you're here? Poke is a friend of mine and I don't like to see her hurting."

A flash of something resembling jealousy coursed through Vidalia and she whipped around to stare at him. "Is she your girlfriend or something? Is that why you're so insistent about this? You want to keep your little tart happy?"

In a flash Jake was at her side, taking Vidalia by complete surprise. When he bent her over his hip and began smacking the seat of her skinny jeans, she yelped loudly. "What are you doing? Stop it! Ow!"

"Poke isn't my little tart. She's the daughter of a good friend of mine and you are disrespecting her and me. That remark was rude and uncalled for with regards to an innocent young girl, and I won't stand for it."

Guilt swept through Vidalia and she started apologizing, even though he hadn't stopped spanking. "You're right, I'm sorry. Please, Jake, I'm really sorry. I shouldn't have said that." If he kept this up, she was sure her jeans would ignite.

"That's better." He stopped and stood her up.

She couldn't help it—she danced on her toes and rubbed her stinging butt. "What's with this caveman imitation?" she asked ruefully. "Are you always this forceful with women?"

"Only with the ones I like," he said, grinning at her.

"Lucky me," she replied dryly.

"If you keep shutting me out, I may get worse," Jake drawled. "Now tell me about Poke, and whether or not you're going to accept her apology. Because if you're not, we have some more talking to do."

"By talking I assume you mean talking with your hand?" Vidalia's eyes narrowed. For whatever reason, she found she didn't resent his spanking her. Attacking the young girl had been a dig at Jake, and a way to make him leave her alone. She'd gotten very good at deflecting people's interest. Jake just didn't respond the same way other people did.

"It's always a possibility." His eyes gleamed down at her.

Vidalia ogled his lean body, the attraction she'd felt for him stirring to life again as she studied his muscled physique. He'd handled her so easily, yet he hadn't hurt her except for a stinging butt, which was already fading into a warm glow that seemed to feed the attraction.

There was no doubt that Jake was a kind man. His concern for Poke—his concern for her—showed her that. Her feelings softened and she sighed. "If it makes you feel better, then I'll go talk to Poke before I leave here. Those cheeseburgers did smell heavenly today. She just caught me by surprise. I don't re-act well right now when it suddenly hits me between the eyes. Especially after the newspapers waged war on dispatchers and public sentiment seemed angry."

Jake reached out and rubbed his big hands gently up and down her upper arms, then leaned in and kissed her on the forehead. "That's my girl," he murmured. "I do remember the newspapers, so I can see why you reacted the way you did. But thank you, she really feels bad."

Vidalia cleared her throat and stepped away, but the warmth of his embrace seeped into her bones. His girl? Being his girl might not be so bad. Not if it made her feel this good when he praised her. She was rather proud of herself that she'd agreed to go talk to Poke, though. Admittedly, she never would have if he hadn't pushed her. "Let's get this finished up, then I have something super exciting to show you."

It wasn't long before the kitchen was sparkling clean, and then Vidalia set her laptop down on the table and hooked up her camera. "Come and see this," she urged.

Jake chuckled and pulled up a chair beside her. Vidalia excited was a beautiful sight. He could barely take his eyes off her as she flipped through the screens to open her pictures up on her laptop.

"This is Victory Falls trail, the one I hiked up today. The falls are simply beautiful," she gushed, pointing at the screen.

Jake had been to Victory Falls many times and knew they were beautiful, but watching the pleasure in her face was even more so.

"You're not looking at the screen," she said, sounding breathless as she turned to face him.

Their heads weren't that far apart and it would have been easy to reach over and capture her lips, but she palmed the side of his face and turned it towards the screen. The next shot that popped up opened his eyes wide. "Bears," he breathed in delight. "You got to see some bears."

She laughed. "Oh yes, a mama and her baby. Isn't the cub cute playing in the water? Watch this." She clicked on one of the photos that was a video clip. Together they watched the bears in the stream, the baby splashing and gamboling about while the mama drank her fill of the fresh water.

Vidalia explained the bears movements that coincided when the kids came into the scene, but she'd kept her camera steadily filming the magnificence of the mama bear when she stood on her hind legs and sniffed the air, and the point at which she hurried her cub into the brush and disappeared.

"And that's when we left too," Vidalia finished. "Just in case she decided to come around and inspect us closer."

"Good call," Jake replied. "I would have left too. You never know how they are going to react. Those two bears look thin, like they are fresh out of hibernation. With them being this close to the Falls, you want to be extra careful about your trash, and also when you're out hiking."

"Maybe we should warn the other cabins around here," Vidalia suggested. "If I had a copier, we could print off a picture of the bears and send it around to our neighbors." She tapped her finger on her lip, thinking.

"Better yet, we could post it at Smokie's. Everyone, even tourists usually stop there on their way up or down the mountain," Jake jumped in. "I have a copier. Why don't I pick you up in the morning and we can make a copy at my house and have lunch at Smokie's."

Vidalia was looking closely at the screen, zooming in on the still shot of the mama bear. "Look there," she said, pointing her finger at something on the bear's ear. "Is that a tag maybe?"

Jake leaned in. "I think you're right. Natural resources and wildlife may have tagged this bear. You might want to send them a picture or call them. They might even know the name of the bear. I'm sure they'll be interested to know she has a baby this year since they've been tracking the bear populations for years. It will also tell them how far she's moved since she was tagged. They like to track their ranges too."

Vidalia's eyes widened. "They name the bears?"

"Some conservationists do," he replied. "So, are we going to lunch tomorrow?"

Vidalia scowled at him. "You have a mind like a steel trap."

Jake smiled, his eyes gleaming. "And don't you forget it."

"Okay, fine. But you don't have to pick me up. I can drive to your cabin if you tell me where it is. No need in coming here and driving back, then driving me back over here."

"That works," he replied cheerfully. "Bring your backpack and wear your hiking shoes. I have something you'll want to take pictures of that most people don't ever see." He figured direct orders might be better than asking to hang out with her tomorrow. Given her penchant for saying no to everything, this might work better. He already had her for lunch, time to up the ante.

Vidalia was certainly intrigued. "And what might that be?" she asked, biting the hook.

"It's a surprise," he replied smugly, popping her on the nose with his finger. It will take about three hours. You want to go before lunch or after lunch?" He had just the spot planned for a hike.

Vidalia considered. "I think before lunch. I'm always up early so I'll come over early. How does 7:00 am sound?

His eyebrows shot up but inside he was more than satisfied. She'd slid neatly into his trap. "That is early, but I can manage it. Are you always up that early?" He figured it had to do with her being unable to sleep, but wasn't going to ask.

She shrugged. "Depends on my schedule. What about you? Don't you work?"

"I'm taking some time off. Remember?" he asked, noticing that she didn't freeze up this time when the subject of her work came up. Maybe they were making some progress.

He'd already decided after yesterday that he wanted to help Vidalia Minton. Not just because he was attracted to her, but because he genuinely liked her. She was smart, sassy, stubborn, sweet, and very, very kind. Which was why she was taking Dani's death so hard. Helping her get past that was important to him. Getting to know the girl he was falling for was even more important.

Vidalia nodded and smiled. "Yes, I do remember now that you said that. She leaned back in her chair and folded her arms, which pushed her breasts up in the thin T-shirt material. "So, what's for dinner tomorrow night?"

Jake swallowed hard when his lowdown buddy reared his head in interest. "Dinner?" he finally managed to croak.

Vidalia lifted an eyebrow. "You've managed to get yourself into my vacation so far with your bossy ways, so now you can pay the piper by doing the cooking. Surprise me with the ingredients I brought with me," she challenged, her eyes gleaming.

Busted!

Jake had to laugh. "You're onto me, aren't you? I should have known you were too smart for your own good."

Vidalia closed her laptop and removed the flash drive she'd downloaded her pictures on. "Just so you know, I don't take orders. I'm only going tomorrow because I want to help spread the word about the bears and because I love beautiful spots I haven't seen yet. So, your spot better be good."

Jake leaned in close to her. "Just so *you* know, I don't respond to threats, no matter how beautiful the lips they come from," he replied softly. "I consider that bratty behavior and I don't put up with bratty."

Her eyes widened and her pink tongue reached out and licked her lips. "I don't consider stating an honest opinion to be bratty."

"But you're not being completely honest, are you?" His buddy below stiffened even more as his gaze chased that little tongue.

"What do you mean?"

"I mean those aren't the only reasons you agreed to go out with me tomorrow. I know better than that."

"You're pretty sure of yourself, aren't you?" She huffed.

Jake chuckled and reached up to slide a lock of soft auburn hair behind her ear. "I'm a man, Vidalia. I like you and I'm pretty darned sure you like me. Even if it's only a little bit. I can work with that." He closed the space between their mouths and pressed his lips firmly against hers.

When Vidalia melted against him and allowed him to explore the sweetness of her mouth, he knew he was right. His entire body responded, his breath quickened, and everything in him stamped her his territory. When she suddenly pulled away and stood up, he forced himself to let her go—temporarily. Disappointment washed over him but he could handle it. He wasn't a lovesick high school boy anymore.

"I-I think you'd better go," she whispered, trembling slightly. "And don't do that again or I won't be going anywhere with you. I'm not in the market for a relationship right now."

Jake stood up. "Okay, Vidalia, I'll go. If this is what you want, I won't kiss you again until you kiss me first. Deal?" He grinned lazily at her.

"That won't happen," she replied firmly. In a few seconds, she was at the front door and holding it open for him.

"If you say so, but I hope you change your mind," he replied honestly. "Good night, Vidalia."

They were both startled when a loud snuffling sound came from around the corner of the cabin.

Vidalia instantly froze in place, her heart rate skyrocketing. "What was that?" she squeaked.

Jake immediately turned around and closed the door firmly, locking it behind him. "I'm not sure, but I think it's a bear," he whispered, flipping off the lights. "But they don't usually come near people, so it doesn't make sense. I'm going to turn off the deck light too," he said, starting towards the patio doors.

"No, wait." Vidalia grabbed his arm and pulled him further into the shadows of the room. "Look."

Stalking stealthily across the deck was a baby bear. "That's not good," Jake whispered. "Don't make a sound, don't move."

As they watched, the little bear stopped to stare curiously at the panes of the French doors.

"Can he see us?" she muttered.

"I don't think so, it's too dark in here and light out there. He can't see in that well, but he might be able to catch our scent and the smell of the food we cooked. They have a keen sense of smell."

The cub stood up on his hind legs and moved in closer to snuffle the glass. They could see his long claws as he scratched experimentally at the door handle.

"Tell me that's locked," Jake whispered, his hair standing on end. Hopefully the curious cub wouldn't be able to turn the knob, but you never knew. Bears were smart—and persistent. "Do you have the keys handy to the pickup?" he asked.

"On the hook by the front door," she whispered back. "Why?"

"Just thinking ahead," he replied, not wanting to scare the crap out of her. But if the mama bear decided they were a threat, she'd be through that mostly glass door like a runaway semi. No way it would stand up under her pummeling. Getting to the truck, which was a lot sturdier than his jeep, would be of paramount importance. And the mother would be here soon—he'd never been surer of anything in his life. He felt Vidalia move and looked down in the dimness. She was making a video again. "Turn that off," he growled, taking the phone from her hands. The light from your phone can point out where we are."

"Oh, damn—sorry."

The bear finally stopped sniffing the door and dropped and rolled around on the deck until finally he went perfectly still and sniffed the air. He'd just turned to head towards the front of the cabin when a black bulk rushed in and slapped him to the ground with a roar.

The cub squalled as the mother bear smacked him again with her huge paw on the back of his haunches, then boxed across one of his ears. Finally, she picked up her bawling victim in her mouth by the scruff of the neck and hauled him around back towards steps that led to the ground.

Jake and Vidalia stayed frozen until it was obvious the bears were gone. Jake heaved a huge sigh of relief. "And there you have mother nature in action. A mother spanking and scolding her baby, and then hauling his little butt back to safety."

Vidalia turned around to face him. "Do you think he ran away from her or something?"

"Fresh out of hibernation, new to the world, you bet. I'm guessing they went to the meadows to look for food and maybe he picked up your recent scent on the path leading around the Victory Falls trail. It's not far up the hill to this cabin. Perhaps he smelled the food scent from our grill and wanted to see what it was."

Vidalia went to the door and flipped the lights back on. "And then mama realized he'd sneaked off," she added with a grin.

Jake smiled down at her. "Oh yeah. Mama bear had to teach baby bear a lesson about running off."

"Do you think they might come back?"

Jake shook his head. "I doubt it, but I'll stay over again just in case."

"There you go again," she mocked, "inviting yourself overnight."

"Do you really want me to leave?"

Vidalia hesitated and he could tell she was pretty uneasy. "No. you can stay. I'm not afraid to say that their visit has made me uneasy. I need to make a trip into town to get some bear spray and some bells. Especially if I'm going to be doing much hiking," she said. "Or just in case junior decides to go exploring in forbidden places—like my living room."

"It would be better if you didn't hike alone right now," he replied with a chuckle. "And be extra careful about your trash."

Her eyebrow shot up. "I'll stick to trails that are well-traveled. Dax left me a list of popular ones. And make lots of noise," she added.

Jake frowned slightly but didn't disagree with her. As far as he was concerned, he intended to keep an up close and personal eye on Vidalia Minton, whether she liked it or not. So, arguing about it was a moot point.

"So, cards, games, or popcorn and a movie?" he asked.

Chapter 5

Vidalia had to admit she had fun watching Harry Potter movies with Jake. She hadn't realized how tuned into the dark aspect of the show she was until he started pointing out the funny parts with random crazy comments. With thoughts of Dani always lurking in the background of her mind like shadows waiting to overwhelm her, the movies seemed to link in with their darkness.

Jake seemed to pick up on some of the vibes she was sending out and would automatically turn to comedy to lighten the tense atmosphere. His sudden question surprised her.

"Do you like watching horror movies?" His keen gaze studied her as the credits to The Deathly Hallows, probably her most favorite, wound down.

She got up to put the movie away and shrugged. "Not really, not the blood and gore type of movies—the ones where teenage kids are always getting sliced up."

He stood up. "Can't say I enjoy those either. But my cousin used to totally love Freddy Kruger and the like. Didn't do anything for me though."

"I don't like horror at all," she confessed, "but I love Harry Potter. It's just a great story of good winning over evil." When he moved closer, she felt her invisible shield begin to raise. She couldn't deny the attraction that sizzled either as she tensed.

"Thanks for the evening, I had a good time," he said softly.

He reached out to snag a lock of auburn hair and smooth it behind her ear. The touch of his fingers on her cheek caused goosebumps. Her breath hitched and she stepped back slightly. "I-it was fun for me too," she agreed.

He looked as if he wanted to say something and changed his mind. With a soft sigh he turned away. "I'm going to sleep in the loft tonight since the cabin is warm. See you in the morning bright and early."

Vidalia watched his firm backside walk away from her and head up the stairs. Broad-shouldered confidence rested on him like a mantle. Disappointment left her deflated. "What did you expect?" She scolded herself as she turned away and went to the door to her bedroom. "You've given him every hands-off sign known to man so why would he want to kiss you goodnight?" Her heart still did a brief flutter as she turned to stare up at the loft. "Good night, Jake," she challenged. Her inner womanly desire for warmth and contact warred with the cautious, embittered dispatcher for superiority.

"You could have kissed me goodnight, brat," he replied as his head popped over the railing. "You lost your chance." He winked and disappeared.

She could hear him chuckle knowingly and she flushed hot with embarrassment. Slamming the door firmly behind her, she stalked to the bed and dragged her pajamas from beneath her pillow. How dare he decide she had to kiss him first? Like that would ever happen. He'd be waiting a damned long time. She completely ignored the fact that she was the one who didn't want a relationship at all.

Huffing, Vidalia got dressed and grabbed the first book of a new mystery series she'd been advised to read. She loved a good mystery for sure. Louisiana Longshot by Jana DeLeon soon had her engrossed in the story of a female CIA assassin hiding out in the little town of Sinful, Louisiana. It was one of the most hilarious books she'd read in a long time and kept her chuckling for the next hour until she finally slipped into blessed sleep.

Sitting on a lawn chair at the edge of the bayou, a storm blowing in and whipping the muddy water in front of her, Vidalia was puzzled. She'd never been in the bayou before. Tense and nervous, she looked around, checking for alligator eye bumps above the water. A sense of impending doom enveloped her propelling her to her feet. Something was bubbling, coming to the surface of the water, yellow tendrils swirling around like delicate spider web fronds. Then she realized it was blond hair attached to a small body dressed in a pink shirt.

It was a child in the water!

Horror and panic assailed her as she leaped forward and grabbed the back of the pink t-shirt and pulled the little body up on the bank. As a dispatcher, Vidalia had training for CPR and she knew she had to try to save this little girl.

The wind was moaning in the cypress trees, the moss dancing wildly around in the branches as Vidalia turned over the still small form. She screamed bloody murder when the face of Dani Owens stared vacantly up at her. No smiles, no laughter shining from happy blue eyes, just ugly death staring back at her, accusing her. "No," she screamed, shaking Dani's body. "You can't be dead. Wake up, Dani, wake up!"

Tears streamed down her face as she was gathered into strong arms and pulled away from the small body lying at the lonely edge of the bayou. Pulling her into another world.

"Wake up, Vidalia," a male voice urged.

Panting, she opened her eyes and Jake's face loomed above her. "I...it...I," she stuttered.

"I'm here, Vidalia," he soothed, brushing her sweaty hair back from her forehead with one large palm. "It's all just a bad dream," his gravelly voice soothed.

She was shaking all over, the last remnants of the ghoulish nightmare fading slowly away. Vidalia's pain and anguish was a giant, unfillable hole in her mind. "She wasn't supposed to die," she cried, "she wasn't supposed to die. I should have saved her."

"I know," he said quietly. "I know how you feel."

Suddenly enraged, she tried to claw her way out of his lap. "No, you don't. You can't know how I feel," she yelled angrily at him. When his arms locked tighter around her, she beat her small fists against his bare chest. "Let me go."

"Settle down now," he replied, grabbing her fists and holding them still.

Vidalia tried to kick him instead. With a wild screech, she kneed him in the stomach as hard as she could. "I said let me up!"

He grunted and put both her wrists in one hand and reached around and slapped her outside thigh with the other. "I said settle down, Vidalia Minton, before I turn you over my lap and settle you down."

"Who the hell are you to tell me what to do?" She glared up at him. His loose hand locked in the back of her hair and held her in place, his smoky gaze licking her flushed face. Her thigh was smarting where he'd slapped it. High-handed ass-hole. she thought furiously. Still, the lips above her were firm, surrounded by the beginnings of new beard growth and hover-ing just out of reach. As if he were tempting her.

Or was being tempted by her.

Either way, Vidalia was mesmerized, her chest heaving as he spoke.

"I'm the man holding you right now, and I'll hold you as long as I feel it's necessary. You're still trembling and shaking like a leaf and I won't allow you to hurt yourself against me, or to stumble and fall if you try to get up and run." His voice was low and determined but not angry. His eyes held shadows of their own as he continued. "I know what it's like to lose a pa-tient, especially a child. It hurts like hell. A pain so bad you can barely face it. It takes a long time to get over that and you usu-ally can't do it alone."

"How do you know?" she whispered in anguish, wanting to believe him, grasping at straws to relieve her own pain as it chased away the rage and settled in.

Jake hesitated, and then spoke. "His name was Hamal, and I lost him on my watch."

"What happened?" Jake was uneasy, she could see it in his face. He didn't want to talk about it. She just couldn't help ask-ing.

"Let's just say I'd saved his life once when his family had been killed by insurgents. He'd been brought into the medical tent with a bullet hole through his shoulder."

"Oh no," she gasped, already channeling the horror of that moment. Poor Jake.

"He followed me around everywhere after that, like a small puppy dog with big brown eyes. He had a ready smile and laugh in spite of what he'd been through. He was an amazing child," he replied gruffly. "I thought I could protect him, but I failed him when he needed me most. It was very difficult to get past."

Vidalia's anger draining left her feeling like a deflated balloon as sympathy took over. She palmed the side of his face. "I'm so sorry, Jake. I'm sure it wasn't your fault. I'm sure you did everything you could to save Hamal."

Jake nodded briefly. "Just remember your own words, Vidalia. You need to apply them to yourself and stop taking all the blame for Dani's death. I know it's hard to do, but you have to or you'll be a basket case stuck in a memory you can't get out of."

His words shocked her. Was he right? "I-I'll try," she finally responded. She wasn't sure how she was supposed to do that. She sat up in his lap and he finally let her go. Being aware of his bare chest under her hand and the hard thighs beneath her bottom was moving in on her senses. "I'm really tired," she said with a yawn and glancing at her watch. "It's only 3:00 am so I'll take a sleeping tablet and try to get a few more hours."

He stood up with her and frowned. "You're still taking sleeping pills?"

She averted his eyes, his knowing stare unnerving her. "Not for much longer," she lied. She was planning on getting a refill—if the doctor would allow it. If not, she'd have to find an alternate method of getting some sleep. If only the nightmares would leave her alone.

"Tonight, you and I are going to have a talk," he promised. "Right now, I'll let you do your thing."

"What kind of talk?" She asked suspiciously.

"About things you can do to help you sleep better and get off those pills. Like seeing a therapist, and other things." His gaze locked firmly on her and she realized he was totally serious.

"It's really none of your business," she replied curtly. Holding the door-knob, she waved a hand to usher him out. "I can deal with this on my own."

Jake walked the few steps to the door and stopped to take her chin in his hand. "No, you can't, you just don't realize it yet. But I'm going to help you anyway, whether you want it or not." Then he grinned lazily and moved his mouth in close. "You ready to kiss me yet?"

Vidalia was sorely tempted, in spite of his irritating avowal that he was going to help her. It kind of warmed her insides a little bit to know that he seemed to care enough to try.

"Ha! In your dreams."

"It'll be a reality soon enough," he promised cheerfully. "Good night then, Vidalia. See you in a few hours."

Vidalia didn't watch him go this time.

JAKE WAS GLAD SHE DIDN'T watch him go up the stairs. He knew he wasn't going to sleep for a while. After throwing on a black t-shirt and his jeans and grabbing a blanket, he let himself out onto the deck of the cabin and slipped into one of the Adirondack chairs out front. It was a bit chilly, but not bad for May. He welcomed the cold fresh air to clear his senses.

Talking about Hamal didn't bring the stabbing pain it used too. Like Vidalia, he hadn't wanted to face the boy's death, knowing he was responsible. It had been a grieving process he'd had to work through, to learn to forgive himself, and admit that there wasn't anything he could have done to prevent it. And like Vidalia, he'd replayed it a thousand times or more in his mind and always came up with the same answer. He was past the nightmares and cold sweats stage every night, but the occasional dream would roust him from his sleep even now. Mostly, he just couldn't get to sleep if his mind was determined to relive it again.

An occasional light mountain breeze tickled the leaves causing them to rustle like whispering voices in the trees. A small crack of a twig here and there signaled the night creatures like the raccoon and the foxes on the prowl. His Rocky Mountain home was as far removed from the dry sands of Afghanistan as you could get, its peace and beauty a balm to his tortured soul. Wrapped snugly in his blanket, he drank in the early morning calm, that time between midnight and dawn before the birds woke up, and found himself drifting off.

His thoughts traveled to Vidalia Minton. She was the first girl who had ever reached his protective, beat-your-chest instincts and tempted his libido into overdrive. Totally used to having her own way though, not to mention beautiful, proud and stubborn.

Too stubborn for her own good.

She needed someone just as stubborn who she couldn't defy all the time and get away with it. He intended to be that man. He dozed lightly in his cocoon, yet still aware of every night sound in that somnambulant state.

It was the early morning birds chattering to each other as the sun began to send exploratory light beams into the shadows of the forest that began to fully wake Jake up. He leaned slightly to one side, relieving some of the pressure on his butt from the wooden slats of the chair and reveled in the warmth of his blanket cocoon while his nose was cold in the chilly air. Slowly he opened his eyes, a ritual he'd enjoy many a morning at his own cabin, to let the day say hello to his senses.

It was going to be a gorgeous day. A small ground squirrel jumped up on the deck and studied him, its little black eyes shining with curiosity as his furry head cocked from one side to the other. A noise from the cabin door startled it and it leaped from the railing and raced back up a nearby tree trunk.

The smell of coffee wafted up his nose as Vidalia stepped out on the deck and walked to the top of the steps. He watched her in her tight black yoga pants topped with a hot pink sweatshirt and brown house slippers with bear eyes and noses on her feet. Seriously?

He hadn't taken her for the fuzzy slipper type, but then again, it spoke to him of a girlish side to her personality. Maybe she was giving out signals unconsciously that she wanted to be protected like a little girl. He was good with that, he thought, grinning to himself.

His eyes traveled up her long legs to the nicely rounded butt and on up to the lush fall of rumpled auburn hair below her shoulders, the sun catching the gleaming strands. Desire set his blood rushing to his manhood.

"Got any more of that coffee?" He asked, finally sitting up straight and letting the blanket fall away so he could stretch.

"Aiee," Vidalia shrieked, dropping her coffee cup and whirling around. The brown liquid sloshed all over the bear nose on her right slipper when the cup shattered. "Where the hell did you come from? You could have told me you were out here," she accused.

"I believe I just did," he replied with a chuckle, rubbing his bristly chin and yawning. "You're up early, it can't even be 6:00 am yet."

Vidalia snorted. "Look who's talking. How long have you been out here?" She bent over to pick up the broken glass. The contents of the cup had already drained through the cracks in the decking.

"For a while," he admitted. "You must really like fuzzy slippers," he added, teasing her as she took the slipper off and shook out the coffee.

"Don't be a hater. What's not to like about fuzzy slippers?" She shot back at him. She headed for the door with the broken cup in one hand and the slipper in the other. "Since this is all your fault, why don't you get a fresh cup of coffee for both of us." She disappeared inside before he could comment.

With a chuckle, he stood up and glanced down at his own bare feet. Folding up the blanket, he took it inside and put on his tennis shoes before pouring them both some fresh coffee and taking it out to the table on the deck. The air was warming nicely with the sun chasing away the last dregs of the night shadows.

When Vidalia came out with pink bunny slippers he almost choked on his coffee. Between laughing and coughing he endured her cheeky stare.

"Having trouble with things going down the wrong hole?" She asked sweetly, crossing her legs and bouncing her foot.

"Uh...yeah...something like that," he replied. "At least those match your sweatshirt." She was definitely sassy this morning.

Her eyebrow arched and her pinkie went up in the air as she sipped her coffee. "Are you a fashion expert now?"

He sat his cup down and leaned towards her, his elbows on the table. "Those slippers do strange things to me," he purred. "They make me want to cuddle you on my lap and rub the softness of the bunny fur...among other things."

It was Vidalia's turn to choke on her coffee. A delicate pink stole into her cheeks as she stood up abruptly. "I'm going to get a shower and get ready for the day. Do you want to fix breakfast or just heat up some egg and cheese croissants in the microwave?"

"I'll be happy to fix some breakfast," he replied, standing up and following her into the cabin with a wolfish grin. Her backside was as delicious as her frontside. Her firm buttocks swayed up and down as she walked, enticing him to reach out and grab her. She certainly was one neat little package, full of sass and vinegar this morning, but he'd gotten in the last word.

Even though she said she didn't want to get involved with him, her body was sending different signals. She was just as attracted to him as he was to her. And the more layers he peeled from his little onion, the more intrigued he became.

He loved those fuzzy slippers; they really did make him want to cuddle her. He made a mental note for the future when he needed to find a gift she'd like.

VIDALIA GASPED IN AWE at the picturesque lake spread out before her. Nestled between tall pine sentinels, the sun was casting its beams between the branches and highlighting the fronds on the glistening water.

It wasn't a huge lake, but it looked old with the gnarled tree trunks of fallen soldiers adorning its edges and the worn footpaths here and there allowing you to get closer and inspect the delicate flowers growing on the green frond bases. Yellow, white, and some pink peeking out here and there created a gorgeous canopy that filled most of the lake. Fairy Lake lived up to its name.

"You like it?" Jake asked, pleased with her reaction. This wasn't a hike often taken in the spring and it wasn't easy to get to. Only the most avid of hikers and those in good physical health were able to make it up the steep incline and sometimes slippery slope.

It was only about an hour for a strong hiker but he'd held back a bit for Vidalia, wanting her to enjoy the entire trail and the reward at the end. He needn't have worried; she'd taken to it like a champ, barely out of breath when they reached the lake. "This is one of my favorite places to come for peace and quiet," he added softly.

Turning to him with shining eyes, she nodded her head. "If you look hard enough, it feels like you can see fairies dancing on the water lilies," she replied reverently. "It's a magical place, I can feel it."

He held out his hand. "I know what you mean," he added gruffly. "Come on, there's a really good spot for pictures just around the other side. And some great seats on the tree trunks of some of the giants who've fallen."

Holding Jake's hand while he helped her over the rough spots sent tingling sensations up Vidalia's arm. It was warm and fully enveloped hers in a firm grasp. There was no denying he made her feel completely safe.

When they reached the other side, she was delighted to see a couple of natural benches had been carved into the wood of two huge trees and sanded off and lightly coated in some type of resin. "Did you do this?" she asked, running her fingers over the smooth surface.

"Maybe," he admitted with a quirky grin. "I used to spend quite a bit of time up here, so I figured I might as well make it more comfortable."

Vidalia saw the shadow flit briefly across his face and knew he was thinking about Hamal. Then he returned to his aggravating self.

"Makes a nice spanking bench too," he joked.

Her eyes narrowed. "Spanked a lot of women up here, have you?" she snarked. Her body heated slightly.

He shook his head, his eyes dancing. "Not a one...yet. You get to be the first." He tugged her towards the bench on the right.

Vidalia dug her heels in. "I don't think so," she protested, unsure of whether he was serious or just fooling around. "What's with this spanking thing anyway?" He got her to the bench and pulled her down to sit beside him. She was relieved he didn't make any effort to pull her over his lap.

"You like fuzzy slippers, I like spanking a gorgeous bottom," he drawled with a lazy grin that set her heart racing.

"You just like throwing your weight around," she protested with a laugh. It was hard not to laugh when he was being so silly. "That could be considered assault with a deadly weapon."

"What deadly weapon?" He feigned mock horror.

She picked up his hand and turned it palm upward. "That deadly weapon," she accused, "it's hard as a board." It was too, it had left her skin stinging like dozens of ant bites.

"It doesn't always have to be that way. Sometimes I can guarantee you would like it," he promised.

She stared doubtfully at him considering the ramifications of his words. It's not like she hadn't heard about sensual spanking. Hell, she'd read a few romance books with a "good girl" spanking in them, but she'd never seriously considered it might be true. They were okay to read though, and some had even left her wondering. The few men she'd dated had never seemed remotely interested in it, even if she had been. Besides, the whole idea was embarrassing to contemplate.

It was one thing to get your butt smacked for punishment, and her parents hadn't minded doing that when they felt she deserved a few swats. But until Jake had smacked her, she hadn't considered it in a relationship.

"Look," he whispered, gently palming her face away from him and towards the lake. "Take a video, quick, before it's over."

Vidalia gasped and brought her camera up, the subject of spanking forgotten for the moment.

Chapter 6

As Vidalia watched in delight, the sun was slowly being eaten by a porous cloud and everywhere the beams shown between the holes and hit the lake, the light flitted off the flowers and lilies making it appear to dance. It only lasted about a minute, just long enough for the cloud to fully pass the sun. She filmed it all, down to the last dancing beam jumping off the water and into the woods on the other side.

"That was incredible," she said slowly. "Why have I never heard of this place before now?"

"Because those who are lucky enough to get to see it, don't want to spoil it," Jake replied. "Tons of people coming up here all the time would ruin the whole place with their trashy disrespect. It's also not very assessable to the average person," he added. "It did have a write up once in one of those travel magazines. Mostly I think it's just that most people go for the easier hikes."

She stared curiously at him, feeling like this was important to him somehow. "Have you ever filmed it?"

He gazed into the horizon and slowly nodded. "I did get the most awesome video once by accident," he confessed. His jaw tensed. "It was raining when I came up here that morning. As I sat here under the tree cover, cold and miserable I might add, the rain stopped and a rainbow end sat on the lake. I've never been to the end of the rainbow before," he joked feebly, clearing his throat. "I can guarantee you there's no pot of gold, or if there was, it was in the middle of the lake and I wasn't going diving for it."

Warmth and understanding raced through Vidalia and she knew instantly that memories of Hamal had driven him to this spot. His attempt at humor was masking the deep emotion he'd felt that morning, and was feeling even now. Impulsively, she covered his large fist with her hand. "The rainbow is the sign of a fresh beginning," she said gently. "A sign of hope for a better future."

His large thumbed slipped out and rubbed the top of her hand. "Yeah...something like that," he replied hoarsely.

"Have you ever seen it again?"

He shook his head. "No, I've tried many times, but it's never come back again." He put his arm around her and tucked her in close to his large frame and they sat there in comfortable silence together.

Vidalia lay her head on his shoulder and sighed contentedly. So much for keeping this man at bay, she thought. He was insidious and addicting. Not to mention full of surprises. Impulsively, she wanted to do something for him.

Before she had second thoughts, she slipped from beneath his arm, laid her camera aside and crawled across his lap. They were sitting in the middle of the bench so there was plenty of room to position herself in the line of fire.

"Show me," she demanded softly, glancing back at him with a nervous grin. Would he reject her? If he did, she would feel like the biggest fool ever. She bit her lip as she felt the flush spreading to her cheeks while he stared down at her in surprise, and then a smile slowly slid across his devilish mouth.

"I'd love to, darlin'," he replied, his eyes eating her up.

One large hand settled around her waist and tucked her in close to his body and the other began rubbing her buttocks. Her body tensed, waiting for that first swat and hoping it wouldn't be too painful.

"Relax," he purred. "This is all about pleasure. You're giving me pleasure by asking for it and I'm giving you pleasure in return by giving it to you."

"It won't hurt at all?" She asked doubtfully.

"Pain can be pleasurable," he murmured. His left hand was kneading the knots between her shoulder blades.

She stiffened, suddenly regretting what she was doing. What in the world was wrong with her? Who in their right mind wants pain? "M-maybe this wasn't such a good idea."

He immediately slapped the seat of her jeans causing her to yelp. "Ouch!"

"Don't give up on me now," he ordered. "The best is yet to come."

His palm was soothing the same spot he'd smacked and the sting dissolved into a throbbing warmth that wasn't unpleasant. She was surprised. "I-I...that wasn't so bad," she whispered finally, enjoying his palm sliding down the backs of her thighs and kneading the tired muscles from their hike. "Ohhh...that feels really good."

He chuckled, his fingers dipping between her thighs and running up the seam of her jeans. "We've barely begun."

Vidalia couldn't help the moan that pried her lips loose when he touched her between her legs. Even through her jeans and panties, she could feel his exploration. When another swat landed under the edge of her buttocks where his fingers had just been, her hips lifted involuntarily in supplication of another caress. And it came, just like magic, causing dancing sensations through her body like the sunlight on the water. Bright, tingling, and blossoming into real desire.

It didn't take a degree to figure out Jake had been right, or where this was headed. She should stop him; she knew she should. Just the same, her hips wouldn't listen to her and when his left hand slid beneath her and opened the snap on her jeans so he could slide them down over her buttocks, she was past caring.

"You're so beautiful, Vidalia," he whispered, leaning down to place a kiss on her lower back. Then he pulled her panties between her butt cheeks and continued the sweet torture of stinging spanks coupled with mind blowing caresses that ending with fingers sliding over her soaking channel and across the bud that swelled and ached for his touch.

"Oh, lord, Jake," she moaned unable to help herself. She wanted this more than anything, she was helpless to stop him. They barely knew each other and she was granting him liberties she'd never let anyone take before. "We shouldn't be doing this."

"Do you want me to stop?" he teased.

"No...no don't stop," she panted. This was uncharted territory for her and she fully intended to complete the ride she knew had to be coming.

His fingers stilled on her bottom. "I don't know, you said you didn't like pain, maybe I should stop."

"Don't stop," she wailed, feeling her reward just out of reach. She reached back and punched his thigh desperately.

"Uh oh...hitting me is against the rules," he tutted. He lifted his hand and swatted a flurry of firm spanks all over her buttocks and then plunged his fingers into her soaking channel before pinching her swollen nubbin.

"Owww...that hurt," she squealed and then fell off the precipice as her body shook with pleasure that had her bucking like a crazy woman. She rode the sweet torture of his hand and fingers until she didn't have a spasm left in her. Then she collapsed.

Chuckling, Jake rubbed her all over her buttocks and thighs, then put her panties and jeans back in place before picking her up and cuddling her on his lap. "You're like wet spaghetti." His voice was complete masculine satisfaction though, she could hear it.

"Do you like spaghetti," she asked with a sudden tired yawn, and to cover her sudden embarrassment.

"I love spaghetti," he teased. "Covered in sauce and easy to eat, what's not to like?"

She blushed furiously as the double meaning became apparent. "I-I..." she stuttered.

He laughed out loud then. "I'm embarrassing you, I'm sorry." He didn't look sorry though.

"No, you're not," she replied, "but that's okay. I have to admit, you were right. It's not easy for me to admit when I'm wrong though, so don't get used to it," she added with a mischievous grin. "Speaking of food, I'm starving. Can we head back to Smokie's now?"

Jake took both her hands in his. "Thank you," he said softly. "You were correct in my reasons for why I come up here. Now this place will have even more special meaning to me."

She blushed and grabbed her camera. "I want to take your picture sitting on your bench," she said, not knowing what else to say. He crossed his legs and put both muscled arms on the tree behind him and allowed her to take several shots.

Finally, he stood up. "Would you like me to take some of you on the bench?"

"Sure." She handed him her camera. They even took a few silly selfies. After he was finished, they made their way around the rest of the small lake, stopping for pictures whenever Vidalia found a spot she liked, then they headed back down the main trail. By the time they got to Smokie's it would be lunchtime.

Vidalia was sensitive to Jake's every movement, her skin tingling wherever he touched her. Never having been so aware of another human being before, she wondered if she was falling in love with the crazy man. He'd made her laugh, he'd made her cry, and he'd sent her skyrocketing into pleasure. She found herself hoping the bears would come back just so he'd stay another night. It's not like she could ask him to, that would just be too weird. How could her feelings change so much in just a few days?

As they trudged down the mountain, she realized that she was thinking less and less of Dani during her waking hours, and more and more about Jake. Was he doing it on purpose? Was he giving her something else to concentrate on in an effort to help her? Most disturbing of all was wondering if he'd want to see her after this was all over. She owed herself this time though, to decide if she wanted to go back to dispatching. That was why she hadn't wanted to be distracted by a relationship with him. Fear of failing another human being like she had Dani was a terrifying reality.

THE AROMA INSIDE SMOKIE'S was heavenly. Jake's stomach rumbled when the smell of roasting meat permeated the air. "Hey, Poke," he said with a grin as they walked up to the counter. "You got some lunch back there for hungry hikers?"

"I sure do," she replied eagerly, her gaze swinging to Vidalia beside him.

Poke was easy to talk to and he could tell the girl was genuinely sorry for any distress she'd caused Vidalia, who accepted her apology with grace.

"Can you post this on your bulletin board?" He asked, handing her the notice he and Vidalia had prepared and explaining the situation.

"Oh wow, I can't believe these great shots you got of the bears," Poke exclaimed. "You rarely have a sighting unless someone goes higher looking for them. I'm surprised they are even down this low."

"It was Vidalia who took the shots," Jake replied.

"We're going to call the parks service and let them know," Vidalia chimed in. "Jake says they sometimes track and name the bears and it looks like this one has a tracker on it."

"Maybe there isn't as much room at a higher level this year," Jake explained with a frown. "Lack of range and food might send them lower."

Poke nodded. "There is an open hunt season planned this year, so that should help."

Vidalia frowned. "People are allowed to hunt bears up here?"

Jake nodded. "Bears populations have grown in the last 40 years and when they have no natural predators, they can start to get dangerous when they come lower and run into civilization. That makes it necessary for everyone's safety, including the bears."

"I see. Sort of like deer season in other states. The herds have to be culled every year because they populate really fast. A lot of people in my state depend on venison to ease their meat budgets during the winter. It can be an acquired taste though. I like the burger and the summer sausage my dad used to have made up, but not much of anything else," Vidalia contributed.

"Poke, I need ya back here," Joe called from the back.

"Be right there," she replied. "I'll get your lunches and bring them to the table," she promised before she hurried off.

It wasn't long before they were biting into the juicy burgers and enjoying hot French fries washed down by ice cold sodas. "Mm mm...delicious," Vidalia enthused, some juice running down her chin.

Jake reached over with his napkin and dabbed the corner of her mouth. "Can't take you anywhere, can I?" He teased. He was delighted to see her enjoying her food. What he'd seen so far hadn't been encouraging as the *wallowing in her misery* sort of appetite had been obvious. He'd been to that address before.

She wrinkled her nose at him. "I can wipe my own mouth...*Daddy*," she retorted with a taunting grin.

Boy did that one word send a direct arrow to his quivering buddy making him stand on end and try to stare at her through his jeans. What the hell?

Vidalia Minton was causing reactions in his body that he simply wasn't used to. Involuntarily his own mouth went with the natural flow her sassy remark had started. "Be careful, little girl. *Daddies* spank naughty brats."

She stared at him, her green eyes wide as a pink flush crept into her cheeks. She looked as shell-shocked as he'd been. Maybe they were both learning some new things about each other. He knew his protective hero streak was as wide as the Sahara Desert, he just hadn't realized how much he enjoyed this sort of teasing and playing around.

At least with Vidalia.

Her eyes dropped and she lent all her personal attention at that point to her food, barely glancing at him. "I'm not a brat," she managed to huff indignantly while devouring an innocent French fry with all the zest of an attacking piranha.

He thought back to a girl named Suzy, a girl with a dependent streak that had looked at him with dollar signs in her eyes and had tried to call him daddy. He knew right then and there a sugar daddy was never going to be his persona. Not that he had a lot of money, but the clingy type hadn't appealed to him. He liked the spirited, independent, feisty type. In fact, the more layers that peeled away from his little onion, the more he liked her.

"That's too bad," he replied softly, his eyes devouring the temper on her face. "I like cute little brats—it gives me a reason to spank."

She chewed on her last burger bite and finally lifted her eyes and studied him, the food puffing out one side of her cheek. God...he was falling in love with this woman.

She swallowed her bite, licked her fingers and then swiped her napkin all over her mouth. "You," she stated emphatically, pointing her delicate forefinger at him accusingly, "are an 1870 throwback. I don't know why I thought I liked you. Don't plan on staying at my cabin tonight I'll be fine on my own," she huffed, pushing her chair back and standing up.

He stood up too. "Vidalia," he said, a warning tone in his voice.

They were both startled when a young man standing at the bulletin board suddenly exclaimed. "Hey, we saw this bear today."

His friend pointed with excitement at the baby. "Yeah, man, that's the same baby. That was pretty cool."

Jake strode over to the two men, Vidalia following. "Where did you see them?" He asked with a frown.

"Up by the falls." His blue eyes were animated, his cheeks almost as red as the head of carrot top curls he sported on his lean, six-foot frame.

His friend was probably a bulky two inches taller with dark hair cropped close to his head, but no less excited. "They were in the same place as this picture," he added.

Jake nodded. "Just be careful, don't try to approach them if you see them again."

"Oh, heck no," Carrot Top assured him. "We wouldn't do that, would we?" His gaze slid to his friend and he nodded in agreement, then they hurried right out the door.

Watching their antics, Jake wasn't so sure. Something about those two seemed a little off, but he couldn't identify just what it was.

"It looks like they are staying in the area, is that normal?" Vidalia asked after they left.

"Not really. They should be at a higher elevation," Jake replied, taking her hand and pulling her away. "We need to make some phone calls this afternoon and try to get this sorted. If something is keeping those bears this low, they need to find out what it is. It puts the bears and everyone else around here in danger. Not to mention visitors and tourists on the trails."

Poke had joined them. "Actually, you all aren't the first ones to mention seeing bears this spring," she added with a worried frown. "You're the only one who has brought in pictures and thought to warn everyone, but a few other hikers have reported seeing a bear. I thought it was strange, but exciting, you know? We all love seeing wildlife. I just didn't think about it being so unusual."

Jake nodded. "Thanks for the info, Poke. We'll tell the parks authority what you've said. "Why don't you jot down the descriptions of those two young men and where they saw the bears, and collect any other information if someone else comes in. Plus, if you remember who has reported it before, and where they saw bears, jot that down to. I'm sure the authorities will be very interested to know."

Poke's eyes lit up. "I'll do that, Jake."

"Poke! I need ya back here!"

"That's Joe, I got to go." Poke rolled her eyes and hurried off.

Vidalia looked up at Jake. "I'm finished with my lunch, but you aren't. I want to look at a few things here in the gift shop, so why don't you eat while I browse? Then we can go back to your place, since you have cell service there, and make those calls."

Jake took out his wallet and handed her two twenty-dollar bills.

Vidalia put up her hand. "Uh uh, my lunch was on the house, remember?"

"It's not for lunch," he protested. "Grab me some of that rocky road fudge they have in the gift shop. Whatever that will cover."

Vidalia's eyes widened and a grin appeared. "You a chocoholic?"

Jake flushed slightly. "Of course not. Well, not like a woman anyway," he teased. "They make it locally and I like to support the business."

"Uh huh...sure...you just don't want to admit loving chocolate because it's a woman thing." She cocked her head knowingly to the side, her eyes full of mischief.

He put both hands in the air in defeat. "Okay, you got me. Just don't tell Dax, I'd never live it down."

She laughed then and Jake was entranced. He hadn't heard her laugh before. It was light, musical, and lit up her eyes from within. He badly wanted to kiss her, but he knew that was impossible. He had to wait for her to kiss him first. Dammit, why had he even said something that stupid?

Mentally he groaned. "My foods getting cold," he growled turning her around and pushing her butt with his hand. "Get, woman, do your shopping."

She shot him a smug glance over her shoulder. "Don't worry, your secrets safe with me. I always guard blackmail material with my life."

Jake watched her as she moved around in the gift area, wolfing down his second burger in record time and finishing off Vidalia's fries. Fishing for his cell phone in his pocket, he located it and pushed Dax's number.

"Hey, buddy, what's up?" Dax's cheerful voice landed in his ear.

"I got her to laugh today and she seems to be enjoying herself," Jake said without preamble.

Dax's voice turned serious. "You of all people know what it's like to present one facade to the world and be lost in a different one in your mind," he replied. "Trust me, Vidalia isn't over this, she needs time and help. She seemed normal here at work too, until she lost her temper and threw a cup of coffee at the wall in the breakroom."

"Wow," Jake replied. "I didn't take her for a hot temper."

"That's just it, she doesn't have one. The stress is destroying her little by little. She's been snapping and snarling at some of our crazy regulars on the phone where she used to be really sweet and understanding. Like the old lady who couldn't find her cat the other day. She told Mrs. Heinz that if she didn't harbor fifteen illegal cats in her house, she wouldn't have to worry about losing one. Then proceeded to tell her to stop calling 911 for non-emergency calls unless she wanted to be arrested for filing false reports."

Jake couldn't help but chuckle. "Sounds like it was a conversation long overdue," he said. "But I get what you're saying, she's not her normal self."

"Sometimes she is, sometimes she isn't."

Jake frowned. "Is it possible part of what she's going through is just simply burnout? It's pretty common among dispatchers, especially 911 dispatchers. There is a lot of life and death trauma calls that come through those phone lines, it happens to the best of them."

Dax sighed. "You're right, of course, and that could very well be part of it. But if she won't see a shrink, she may not get any better at this point. I know she's up there trying to help herself, and that's good, but I just don't think it's going to be enough."

Jake cleared his throat. "Okay, I have to let you go. It looks like she's about done with her tourist shopping. I'll try to talk to her again, but she shuts down every time I say anything about it. She refuses to discuss it."

"Where are you at?" Dax asked curiously.

"At Smokies. We took a hike this morning and stopped in here for lunch."

"At least she's letting you spend time with her, that's encouraging," Dax enthused.

"So far, so good. Later, buddy." Jake rang off and waited for Vidalia to finish her purchases at the counter. His thoughts drifted to the time they'd spent at Fairy Lake. It felt like she liked him, and better yet, trusted him. Granted, their relationship was in its early days even if she didn't call it a relationship. She was a mass of contradictions. He would never have believed she would voluntarily lay herself over his lap like that, yet she wouldn't trust him with her life-shattering experience.

Jake considered his options. He'd try to give her a few more days to open up willingly, but if she didn't do it soon, then he'd resort to other means. The wound she was protecting would only continue to fester until something was done about it.

He stood up as she approached the table and handed him a bag. "Did you get everything?"

She smiled up at him. "Of course. I even bought some fudge for myself so I could help support the local candy makers," she replied with a chuckle. "And I bought a book about bears to study."

"Come on then, let's get going," he said, smiling back at her. "We have calls to make, another short hike before dinner, and you can help me make lasagna at my place to eat tonight."

Her eyes narrowed at him. "Is that a request or an order?"

"Which do you prefer?" He loved the indecision in her eyes. No matter what she said, he was determined she would eat at his place tonight, even if he had to flatten one of her tires to do it. But he was pretty sure she wanted to; she was just stubborn.

"Homemade German chocolate cake for dessert," he added as an incentive.

That put her over the edge, her eyes lighting up. "If you're cooking, I'll stay and eat," she relented. "Lasagna happens to be a favorite dish of mine."

"I knew you couldn't resist the chocolate cake, admit it." He waggled his eyebrows at her. "I've got you pegged."

"Don't get overconfident, 1870, I can always change my mind," she said with a chuckle as she preceded him out the door.

They both waved at Poke as they left and he opened the door to his jeep and helped her inside, his possessive streak in full mode. He even patted her bottom as she hopped up the steps, ignoring the *if looks could kill* glare, she shot him.

They had both driven to his place this morning so she'd have a way home tonight. It was what she'd wanted, so he'd agreed even though he knew he'd be following her back to her place anyway. No way was he letting her stay alone in the cabin while those bears were still around.

"No copping a free feel," she scolded, but her eyes were twinkling at him.

"It's not free, it's costing me a big slice of my mom's home-made chocolate cake," he said with relish.

Her mouth dropped open. "What? I thought you made the cake!"

"I never said I made it." He grinned unrepentantly.

"You...you...," she sputtered, then she laughed and shook her head. "You got me there."

"I've got you everywhere," he replied smugly. "And I'm not letting go."

Chapter 7

Vidalia watched the incorrigible Jake as he rounded the front of the jeep. He'd tricked her neatly into dinner she had to admit. Being on her guard in the future would be paramount or he'd have her emotions completely tied up in no time.

Would that be so bad though?

"Shut up," she ordered her conscience. The faint scent of his wintergreen aftershave lingered where he'd leaned across and neatly snapped in her seatbelt before she could protest. She hadn't even bothered to say anything because he'd already won this round. Next time she'd be ready for him. The touch of his body across her breasts had left her nipples tingling even through their jackets. If he'd just turned his head towards her, she could have kissed those firm, smug lips.

A full-body shiver hit her as she realized how much she wanted that. She gave him a side eye as he climbed in beside her, all male strength, sexy gray eyes, and the cutest satisfied grin ever still adorning his face. The man was dynamite wrapped in a muscled male package. She'd never been so aware of someone before. Even her toes were tingling.

When they arrived at his cabin, she was surprised to see that it was much bigger than Dax's. It was about a quarter mile off the main road and nestled among the tall pines like something you would see in a travel magazine.

An oversized carport stood behind the house and to the right on the property, housing a nice-sized cabin cruiser. He must like boating. A large storage building was on the left, leaving plenty of room in between to host a covered concrete patio that was empty at the moment. Probably for guests, she surmised.

"This is gorgeous," she breathed in awe. "Did you build this by yourself?"

He pulled into the gravel drive that sat in front of the two-car garage and turned off the engine. "Not all of it," he replied. The main cabin was already built, as was the boat shelter and part of the storage building. I added some rooms, then added the garage and put up the outside pavilion." He pointed to the additions as he spoke. "I also increased the size of the deck in the front and added one completely around the cabin," he added proudly. "You like it?"

Vidalia nodded. "I love it. It's beautifully done and blends in with the forest around it so well. I can see why you live here as much as you can."

"Well, I have internet service here since it's a lower elevation," he replied. "I wanted that in case I decided to do something that allowed me to work from home. Plus, I didn't want to be too far from civilization. If I did get snowed in, the snow plows would get the roads cleared more quickly."

Vidalia opened her door and climbed out as he came around to help her. "They don't close this canyon off in the wintertime?" she asked.

He took her hand and pulled her toward the front door. "Not normally. Mom and Dad have been staying up here for years and it doesn't close much unless the ice builds up really bad on the roads. Then snow chains are required."

Jake opened the front door and ushered her into the cozy warmth inside. Vidalia could see immediately that it was a man's domain, but it was still beautiful. There were no designer pictures of bears on the wall or pillows in the comfy-looking recliners in front of the fireplace. There wasn't even a sofa, just a broad coffee table in front of the two chairs near the fireplace. The huge cream rug that filled most of the floor space would feel good on bare feet.

A cabinet with stools on the left side of the room separated the kitchen area from the living room. Lights hung from the ceiling in the middle of the cabinet that contained a sink setup which she assumed was for cleaning vegetables and stuff. Against the wall was the main sink, stove with microwave, and refrigerator. A table with six chairs was on the left near a patio door that she could see part of the side deck through.

"Come on, I'll give you the tour," Jake said proudly, pulling her towards the broad doorway at the back of the room. "Down here is the master bedroom with a bath, a guest bathroom, and my office. Plus, the staircase to the upstairs." He pointed upwards when they came into the hallway. "Up there are two more bedrooms and another bathroom."

"And not a doily in sight," she teased.

He grinned lazily at her. "I'm not the doily type. I figure when I find the right girl, she can help me with the finishing touches. I just have the basics covered for now, and some things are still a work in progress, like the kitchen cabinets."

Vidalia's breath hitched. *Whoever the right girl is will be a lucky girl,* she thought.

He turned into the first room to their right and ushered her into his office. "Oh, I love your desk," she said in delight. "It takes up half the room."

"This back half of the house is built on," he replied. "I made the desk myself because I wanted plenty of room."

"I like the way you built the shelving into the wall," she enthused, eyeing the shelves behind the desk which were mostly empty.

"I like to read," he replied simply. "I imagine I'll have it full eventually."

On the wall to the outside, a large picture window gave her another view of the deck. "I love all the windows," she said softly, admiring the view. A window seat had been built in with a cushioned top that she curiously lifted up. Inside were neatly folded plush blankets.

"In case you want to cuddle up in the chairs and read," he said in response to the question in her eyes. He pointed behind her where two overstuffed chairs set complete with pillows and footstools. The wall behind the chairs also had built-in bookshelves, bare of course.

"Ah, a study slash library," she joked. "I like it. And the rest of the house?"

"This way," he said, and her ushered towards the stairs.

After he'd finished showing her the upstairs, they ended up back in the study where Jake sat down at his desk and opened his computer. "Time to look up some phone numbers."

Vidalia sat in the window seat and watched the tree squirrels outside. The wind had picked up and the sunlight had dimmed from bright and warm to clouds drifting in, their full dark bottoms heavy with the portent of thunderstorms. The day was slowly turning darker and she shivered. The weather report for the day had predicted light drizzling rain towards evening, but nothing heavy. She'd always hated thunderstorms, even more so now.

Jake's voice on the phone faded away as her thoughts of that day crept in like a thief determined to steal her sanity.

It was Vidalia's ability to empathize that made her so sensitive to other people and their emotions. From the first cry for help from Dani's frantic voice she'd been drawn into the canyon with the little girl. Thunder was crashing in the background and the harsh downpour of rain filtered in like static behind her pleas for help.

"You have to climb, Dani. You have to get higher, honey. You can do it; I know you can. Look around you. Do you see anything to grab onto?"

"I-I see a big tree root, but it's so high. I-I'm so cold, I can barely move."

"You have to try, Dani," she urged. "You have to get higher than the water."

There was no answer. "Dani? Dani? DANI?"

All sounds from the phone ceased. The line was silent. No rain, no thunder...and no Dani.

Vidalia's head ached; her heart hurt so much she thought it would burst. When Jake's hand touched her shoulder, she nearly jumped out of her skin.

"Vidalia? Are you all right?" he asked softly, turning her to face him. He glanced out the window at the gathering clouds and the winds whipping the tree's branches around, immediately understanding the words she couldn't speak. "Come here," he said gruffly and gathered her into the safe haven of his strong arms and began rocking her.

"They...they said there was nothing more I could have done than I did...but there had to be," she said brokenly. "There just had to be. I can't believe I lost someone on my watch...it was so senseless."

"It would have helped to take the stress debriefing," he replied gently. "You need to talk about it. Observe it from another person's viewpoint." He lifted her chin. "I'd like it very much if you'd talk to me about it."

Vidalia shook her head. "I can't talk about it." How could she explain that if she talked about it, she would diminish Dani's death? The little girl with blond hair and laughing eyes would fade into another statistic and be forgotten. She deserved to be haunted by it, she'd failed in her job.

"In our kind of jobs, we meet death head-on at times, and in all forms, old, young, rich or poor," Jake tried again. "Death is no respecter of age or money, and it can happen when you least expect it, especially for us because we're on the front lines. Losing a child is the worst death of all, and we always second guess ourselves."

Vidalia stiffened and stared at him. "I don't want to talk about it, Jake. I came up here to put it behind me and move on. Talking about it will just bring it back to life, and I don't want to relive it all over again."

"Except that you can't forget about it," he argued. "It won't go away until you face it and stop blaming yourself."

"I'll never stop blaming myself, but I do want to stop thinking about it all the time," she replied tiredly. "That's why I agreed to a couple of weeks off. I just want to think about something else, and my job reminds me of it, every minute of every day."

Jake sighed. "Are you thinking of quitting your job?" he asked.

"Yes," she finally admitted, pulling away from him and getting up from the window seat. "I'm not sure I'll be going back, but I don't know what else I want to do either. Another reason I took some time off, to plan a possible new future."

"What else have you thought of doing?"

"Nurses training maybe?"

Jake snorted. "Out of the frying pan and into the fire, right?"

"Something like that," she replied ruefully. She moved to the chair in front of the desk and sat down. "So, what did you find out? Anything interesting?"

Jake studied her through narrowed eyes, the storm brewing outside behind him plainly visible through the window. She held her breath wondering if the stubborn man would let it go. A part of her wanted to confide in him, but she was afraid to open the door to the maelstrom of emotions that would require. Keeping an iron grip on that door seemed to be all that was holding her together these days. She heaved a sigh of relief when he finally nodded his head and stood up.

"All right, Vidalia, we'll play it your way for now, but this isn't over."

"It's over as far as I'm concerned," she replied, determined to have the last word. It was vital that he understood that or she wouldn't hike with him again, or do anything with him again. She just wanted peace and quiet.

JAKE MOVED TO THE DESK and sat down in his office chair, keeping an eye on Vidalia as he did so. She may think it was over, but he knew it wasn't.

When he'd looked over and found her zoned out, it hadn't taken him two seconds to put her stillness and the encroaching weather outside together to figure out why she wasn't listening to him or responding to his call. As long as she refused to let Dani go, she would never be free.

"There's a ranger assigned to this area and he's already gotten some reports about the mother bear and her cub," he explained. "Although the sows with cubs are usually the late bloomers in coming out of hibernation, they usually either move up higher, or stay higher."

"What do you mean late bloomers?"

"The boars usually begin appearing around the middle of March, and then the sows without cubs, and finally the winter mothers around the middle to late end of April. Which is right in the time frame we are in."

"So, our mama is a late bloomer," Vi said. "I wonder why they come out so late?"

Jake smiled at her. "Read your book and find out. It will tell you why."

His cell rang and Jake picked it up. When he finished the call, he grinned over at her. "That was the ranger and he said the mama bear's name is Sushi because they first spotted her eating trout from a mountain stream. She does like to stay lower in elevation for some reason, but she's not been spotted this low before."

"Sushi?" Vi wrinkled her nose. "That's not a good name for a bear. It should be cuddles or something like that. They were able to enlarge the trace tag I take it?"

Jake nodded. "Yes. And they've given you the honor of naming the baby since yours is the first picture they've received of them together."

"Really? I get to name the baby?" Vidalia asked, her eyes shining with excitement.

He laughed. "They also want you to sign a waiver allowing them to use the photos in whatever writeups they do with it."

Vidalia jumped up. "Of course, I'll sign it, that's amazing! I love that I get to name the baby. When do they need the name?"

Jake came out from behind the desk. "He said he'd come by your cabin sometime this week, but he'll call first."

"Did you give him my phone number?" She shot him a frown. "I don't have cell service at Dax's cabin."

"He'll call me and I'll let you know," Jake promised. "Now let's get busy with that lasagna. We'll have to do the short hike I had planned another time, since looks like rain outside." He took her elbow and steered her out of the office and into the kitchen area. The first thing he did was to close the blinds in the windows and on the patio door, then put on some music to drown out the increasing noise outside. With a fire going in the fireplace, it was snug and cozy.

In spite of her protests that she didn't cook, Jake found Vidalia to be adept in the kitchen. While the thunderstorm raged outside, they had fun together in spite of nervous glances towards the patio. Sometimes a lightning flash would peek in through the edges of the blinds and she'd tense up, but by the time dinner was over and they were enjoying chocolate cake, the rain had passed.

"That was delicious," she said with a sigh. Sitting in front of the fireplace in one of the comfortable recliners, she rubbed her tummy in satisfaction. "You can cook for me anytime. And tell your mother I need her chocolate cake recipe."

Jake reached over from his chair and covered her hand with his large palm. "You're not so bad yourself, you helped with it," he replied grinning over at her. "I'm about to fall asleep, I'm so full."

"I know what you mean." Vidalia yawned.

When Jake's cell phone rang from the depths of his pocket, he frowned. It was the ranger again. When he hung up, he looked over at Vidalia. "That was the ranger. He received a report of a bear going through some trash at one of the rental cabins not far from where you are."

Vidalia frowned. "But who would leave trash out? Even I wouldn't leave trash out and I don't know much about bears. In Missouri, we never had food in our tent or trash out because of raccoons and other curious creatures when Dad took us camping. It's just something you don't do."

Jake's mind flitted to Carrot Top and his friend with a frown. "I don't know, but someone did. I just hope the bear doesn't attack a person. He wanted to make sure you took extra precautions while you're here."

"That was nice of him but I'm sure I'll be fine," Vidalia replied as she stretched and yawned. "Time for me to head back, it's getting later than I want to be out on the roads."

Jake got up and went to the door to peer out into the night. There weren't as many stars as normal, which meant there was still some cloud cover hanging around. The band of thunderstorms predicted could suddenly produce another one, which made him uneasy because the wind was already picking up. "Why don't you just stay here tonight," he said finally, watching her as she gathered her backpack and phone.

"I appreciate the offer, but I'll be fine." She hesitated at the door, and then smiled at him. "Thanks for the company today, and the good food. I'll see you tomorrow if you're still game to hike Killer Alley."

His arms folded across his broad chest. "I wouldn't miss it, but if it's raining, we won't go hiking."

"If it's raining, I'll be going into town," she replied. "It will be my chance to get some things I forgot to bring."

"Let me know if you do, okay?"

She gave him the stink eye. "You know, I have functioned well on my own long before I met you. What makes you think I can't now?"

He knew she could, but Jake was reluctant to even let her out of his sight. "You're an accident just waiting to happen," he finally teased her. Realizing he really felt that way made him more uneasy. There was no doubt in his mind that Vidalia was a powder keg just waiting for a match. He wanted to be there when she blew. PTSD was a very real thing. Even if she hadn't been there in person with Dani Owens, she was having flashbacks in her mind. Maybe even picturing herself right in the scene, helpless and unable to do anything about what was happening, creating the nightmares that were robbing her of restful sleep. She needed help. If she wouldn't allow him to help her willingly before her vacation was over, he might have to take more drastic action.

He watched the taillights of Dax's truck as it carried her away, his sense of unease growing. The wind was building again. Making a decision, he went into the house and grabbed his backpack. After stuffing it with a change of clothes and some beer, he headed out to his jeep.

The wind had really picked up now and he knew another thunderstorm was on its way. Thinking of Vidalia in her cabin alone made his gut clench. He was officially inviting himself over for the night at her place—*again.*

About the time he hit the turnoff for her lane, a huge streak of lighting split the sky and a few seconds later, what sounded like a sonic boom went off. That meant the lightning had been close.

"Damn," he muttered to himself as he navigated the narrow lane. The heavens had literally opened up and sent sheets of rain coursing down so hard he could barely see. Another boomer lit up the night sky as he pulled up beside Dax's truck and ran from his jeep to the overhang of the porch like a jackrabbit. He was still soaked.

He knocked loudly on the door so Vidalia would hear him over the storm. When he tried to peer in the crack of the window blinds beside the door, he couldn't see much but the darkness and a dim light on the stove, At least the electricity wasn't out.

"Vidalia!" He shouted above the noise of the falling rain. "Vidalia, let me in. It's me, Jake!" Still no answer.

Feeling truly concerned, he ran around to the patio door where they had seen the bears. The blinds were half closed but in the dim light inside he could see a dark shape on the floor in front of the door. Rubbing the water off one window pane he finally realized it was Vidalia curled into a fetal position on the rug. "Oh my god," he swore softly. "She must be terrified." He pecked frantically on the glass. "Vidalia!"

In a lightbulb moment, he raced to Dax's truck, opened it and checked in the glovebox. Dax had said he kept an extra key in there in case he ever locked himself out. Quickly he found it in the bottom beneath the truck manual. Returning to the front door, his fingers chilled from the cold rain, he finally inserted the key into the lock and let himself in.

As wet as he was, Jake didn't want to pick her up and get her wet too. Faster than he'd ever disrobed in his life he tore his clothes off, dumped them by the door, grabbed some clothes from his pack, then dragged them on. Then he ran to the prone figure on the floor.

She fought him when he touched her. "No, let me go!"

He managed to get her off the floor and into his arms. Then he sat down with her on the couch and threw the blanket lying there over both of them, rocking and crooning. "I've got you, Vidalia, I've got you. It's me, Jake."

The vacant look in her eyes worried him, knowing she was in a private hell that only she could see. He'd been there a few times too. Beneath the covers he stroked her arms, warming both of them together. He cursed himself for letting her leave alone. He should have known the rabbit hole she was falling down would eventually bottom out beneath her.

Jake wasn't sure how long they had sat there like that, but the storm's fury began to pass and it was quieting down outside. Finally, Vidalia stirred in his arms and he watched awareness creep back into her eyes. She was coming back.

"You okay?" he asked softly, his thumb brushing down the curve of her face.

She tried to sit up. A wobbly hand pushed the covers down as she looked around. "What happened?" She croaked. "And where did you come from?"

"Why don't you tell me what happened?" He instructed softly.

Chapter 8

A wary look crossed her face. "I think I'd like to start a fire," she replied, evading his question. A shudder quivered through her.

Ignoring her comment, he gave her a stern look. "What happened, Vidalia?"

"Nothing," she bit out. "Now let me up."

"That's not going to happen until you give me some answers," he replied frankly.

She stared defiantly at him, her eyes huge in her pale face. She folded her arms over her chest in an unconscious desire to withdraw from him, if not physically, then mentally.

"Let me tell you what happened, since you aren't willing to admit to it." He had one long arm around her butt, his fingers holding the back of her jean's waistband, and the other hand on her outside thigh. She wasn't going to get away from him, and he knew she would try. "You zoned out again for the second time today. When the lightning hit, you went into that canyon with Dani Owens, didn't you?"

Her face flushed. "It's none of your business, Jake. I want you to leave."

"That's not happening either," he replied, his eyes narrowing. "You can't keep pretending this isn't happening. These flashbacks are going to get worse if you don't get some help."

"What flashbacks," she scoffed. "I was never in that canyon, so I can't flash back to something that isn't real. Maybe you have PTSD but I don't."

"It's real in your mind," he said simply. "Look, I'm no therapist, but I've seen one who deals with trauma victims and they have some interesting theories."

"Ha! I'm not a victim."

"Of course, you are," he argued. "You're as much a victim as Dani was because you blame yourself. And until you stop doing that, your mind is going to go with that and help you be a victim. What doctors know about the brain could fit on the head of a pin, as one specialist once told me. But the way you view things yourself can have a huge impact."

"I'll never stop blaming myself," she echoed dully. "I should have been able to convince her to get to higher ground. I should have been more forceful, more calming, more...more...something. Anything to save her life. That little girl is dead, Jake, and it's my fault."

Her dry-eyed, wild stare concerned him, she seemed so positive. "No, it wasn't your fault. The only one who thinks it was your fault is *you*." Jake ran his fingers through his hair, frustrated, and tried another tack. "Besides, how do you know she didn't try? Maybe she lost the cell phone connection while she was trying, but it was too late. "You aren't God, Vidalia. You don't have all the answers, and you have to stop blaming yourself as if it was all cut and dried."

"I know I'm not God, but...but..."

"Have you listened to the tapes?" He interrupted.

"Yes," she yelled, "I've listened to them!"

"And can you think of anything you would have done differently?"

Her tense body slumped. "N-no... but..."

"Anyone can panic, and Dani was no exception," he said gently. His hand moved up her back, caressing and soothing her tense muscles. "You have to forgive yourself and move on. Have you mourned for her? I mean cried and grieved for her loss?"

"Have I cried? No. But I grieve for her, every hour of every day and every nightmare that I come alive in. She haunts me and I can't stop wishing I'd been there to save her in person. I *should* have saved her."

The anguish in her green eyes was heartbreaking as Jake watched her finally talking.

"The storms bring it back even more. One of the things I wanted to do on this trip was to go Rangers Pass and see it for myself. Maybe even when it's storming."

Jake frowned. It sounded more like Vidalia was wallowing in and deepening her pain by thinking viewing the pass would make a difference. "There is no way you can recreate those circumstances, not without putting you in extreme danger. The flash floods that come through there are exactly what Dani got caught in."

"Why do you think I came here at this time?" She argued. "Thunderstorms have been predicted all week this week. And you know as well as I do how they can come up suddenly."

"What makes you think you can handle it when I just found you curled up on the rug?" He demanded incredulously. "And you zoned out earlier today, don't bother denying it. You would get out there and PTSD would hit you and you'd be helpless!" His voice had risen an octave. "You can't do it; I won't allow it."

"It's not your right to tell me what I can't do," she yelled right back at him. "You're not my boyfriend, or husband, or anything!"

"I'll tell you what I am," he gritted through his teeth and leaned into her face. "I'm a friend who cares about you, a man who wants to be your boyfriend, maybe even a husband down the road. That gives me some cred as far as I'm concerned, and with that cred comes the right to spank your stubborn little butt if I think you need it."

She scrambled off his lap but he grabbed her wrist and held onto her while moving to the middle of the couch.

"Don't you dare touch me," she shrieked, clawing at the hand that held her.

"Oh, I'm going to touch you all right," he replied, his other hand reaching up and unsnapping her jeans, then dragging them down partly over her hips. Then he yanked and she tumbled down and across his lap where he finished shoving her jeans down, along with her panties, to mid-thigh, revealing a nice target area. And then he sat fire to her ass.

Vidalia shrieked and yelled all sorts of obscenities with arms and legs flailing in every direction, as much as her legs could with the jeans holding them together. But Jake was through being mister patient guy. "There comes a time when talking just doesn't get through to a stubborn brat," he scolded. "I've been patient, I've been understanding, I've let you have things mostly your own way, but not this time. This ridiculous plan of yours is *not* going to happen, not on my watch."

After her bouncing butt cheeks were a nice cherry red, he paused and rested his palm on the hot, soft skin. She was crying now, whether it was for Dani or just because he was roasting her butt, he didn't know. Either way, it couldn't hurt. Tears were healing.

Stealing his heart against her sobs, he asked. "Are you listening to me, Vidalia Minton?" Her little fists were balled against the sofa cushion and her body was tense. With his left hand, he rubbed her back gently.

"I-I hear you."

Her reply was muffled but he heard it. He reached over and turned her face gently up towards him. Tears were streaming from her eyes and her face was flushed. "Are you going to pay attention to what I'm saying and give up this crazy idea?"

She glared mutely at him and he took that to mean they weren't finished yet. "All right, it's your ass. I can keep this up all night." He laid into her again, concentrating on the tops of her thighs this time until she yielded.

"Okay, okay! Just s-top," she finally wailed.

That was good enough for him. Maybe she meant it, maybe she didn't, but at least she'd have something to think about. Maybe the pain in her ass might keep her from going ahead with her terrible plan when and if she actually decided to do it. He pulled her upright and turned her over, snuggling her into his shoulder while she sobbed. On an impulse, he told her, "If you want, I'll take you to Rangers Pass, but not in the rain. That's just too damned dangerous."

STARTLED AT HIS SUGGESTION, Vidalia tried to get herself under control. She hated crying, always had. It gave her a headache and her eyes puffed up like she'd had an allergic reaction. She hadn't meant to let her secret plan slip out like that, but now that it had, she'd really put her foot in it. Her ass burned worse than a sunburn ever could, and she'd had a few of those in her life. What she wouldn't give for a soothing bottle of aloe vera sun lotion about now.

Grabbing at his words like a lifeline, she peeked up at him and tried to sit up. She grimaced at the roughness of his jeans on her tenderized bottom. "Do you really mean that?" she asked, searching his strong face. Tapping down the urge to punch him was difficult, but she managed. Her position right now was too precarious and she didn't want to feel any more of his board-like hand on her nether regions.

"If you really think it will help you, then yes," he replied.

His eyes had lost that granite expression and softened. Obviously, he didn't think it would, but he was willing to compromise. It was the best she was going to get and she knew it. If she was honest with herself, she'd been terrified at the thought of going to the pass alone, especially in the rain, and had had her own doubts as to whether she could do it. She just knew she had to do something.

She swiped her sleeve across her eyes and her face, soaking up some of the embarrassing tears as best she could. "T-thank you," she said, her words wobbly. Reaching down she tugged at her panties bunched inside her jeans and tried to pull them up while leaning from side to side.

"I can help with that." Jake stood up, taking her with him, then reached around and slipped her panties over her bright red mounds, giving them a satisfied pat before doing the same with her jeans.

"You don't have to look so proud of yourself, 1870," she groused, feeling a little sassier now that she was covered. "You had no right to do that."

"I can do it again," he warned, his eyes narrowing down at her.

She opened her mouth to say no you can't, when she saw the light of battle creep back into those gray orbs. She huffed instead and walked stiffly to the kitchen for a bottle of water. She purposely ignored the male chuckle behind her. After taking a huge swallow, she turned around and ran right into his hard chest, some of the water sloshing out between them. "Damn," she muttered, staggering back slightly. "Do you have to sneak up on me?"

He held her steady by her upper arms and grabbed the neatly folded towel off the cabinet and brushed the water off. "Sorry, it's an old habit," he replied ruefully. "You got another one of those?"

She stepped away and motioned to the fridge. "Help yourself." Heart racing, she turned and headed into the bathroom to survey the damage to her face. Wrinkling her nose in the mirror, she decided it wasn't too bad. Her eyes were definitely brighter with red rims around them, but not that bad.

On an impulse, she turned around and slid her clothes down to inspect her bottom. "Ouch," she grumbled softly as she placed her cool hand on the hot skin. Picking up the lotion she'd set on the sink, she poured some in her hand and then gently rubbed it into the red flesh. "Oh, geez," she whispered to herself. "That feels good."

Away from his overwhelming male presence, she was able to think more clearly. Okay, so maybe he was right, maybe it was a stupid idea. He was also right about zoning out becoming more of a thing.

At first, it had been people clicking their fingers in front of her face and saying something like *"earth to Vidalia"*, which had seemed funny, but now it was more than that.

She remembered driving home and hurrying into the cabin trying to beat the rain, and then going to the window to pull the blinds down when a huge sonic boom had deafened her ears, Light had lit up the outside for a split second and the angry trees had seemed to close in on her, their branches waving in her face and a sense of urgency overwhelming her. Curling up on the ground, she feared for her life, wanting to get to the little girl she knew was fighting to live amongst mother nature's fury. But how could she? She felt so helpless, so incapacitated. Dani was going to die and there was nothing she could do about it.

Then Jake's face had swam into her vision and she'd grasped it like a lifeline to sanity, finally coming back to reality. She sighed, her hand trembling as she picked up the hairbrush and pulled it through her tangled locks. What if she did that out in that ravine? Jake was right, she knew it. She just didn't want him to be right.

Gathering her courage around her, she opened the door to the bathroom. Even if he was right, he didn't need to be spanking her. Her butt didn't belong to him. Even if it *did* belong to him, he didn't need to be spanking it.

When she returned from the bathroom, Jake was propped up on the couch with pillows and another blanket he'd apparently robbed from one of the loft beds.

"Inviting yourself to stay overnight again I see," she mocked, shaking her head. His hands were behind his head and a fire was beginning in the fireplace. The red long-sleeved t-shirt strained against the muscles of his arms and she could clearly see the six-pack in his taut stomach. Most deadly of all was the lazy grin on his firm lips.

"I think it would be best," he drawled. "Care to join me? It's nice here in front of the fire."

Wanting to and not wanting to, her hands fought her internal battle by twisting her own t-shirt between her fingers. "What part of I don't want to get into a relationship do you not understand?" She asked finally, scowling at him.

He sat up and lifted the blanket to entice her into his cocoon. "The same part that keeps telling you that you need to talk," he replied, "but you don't listen any better than me in that regard."

"I just did talk," she grumbled, her feet moving of their own accord towards a man who appeared to meet her stubbornness head on. With a grudging respect, she relented and sat down beside him. "Talking it to death won't change anything," she muttered as he slid his long arm around her shoulder and pulled the blanket over their laps. "And it won't bring her back."

He cuddled her in close and they both sat staring at the fire until he finally spoke. "Hamal was a little six-year-old boy, full of life, happy, and running around like a mad whirling dervish. Once his shoulder healed, he was always underfoot, always curious in spite of the loss of his family. The camp director was trying to find some of his relatives but hadn't been successful.

He paused and Vidalia pictured a black-haired boy with eager brown eyes and already felt the pain of knowing he was going to die. Her throat tried to close up but she swallowed and kept still.

Finally, Jake went on. "It was hot that day in the sandbox, not a breath of fresh air to be had. We were getting a steady stream of wounded and Hamal wouldn't stay out of the way. I yelled at him more harshly than I should have, and he left the medical tent. I didn't know where he'd gone and didn't have time to check on him."

He shifted slightly in his seat and Vidalia could feel his body tense. Her lips tightened in sympathy and she took his hand quietly in hers and squeezed.

"I heard someone yelling stop outside, and calling his name, so I rushed out of the tent and found him in the middle of a crowd that had moved completely out and away from him. He was walking towards me as if he was unsure of himself because everyone was yelling at him. I could tell he was confused.

Then he pointed to the vest he had on, telling me that he had found his uncle in the desert not far from the camp and he'd given him this beautiful vest. He wanted to show the vest to his new friends before going home with his new-found relative and his uncle had approved.

"Oh my god," Vidalia breathed.

Jake nodded his head. "Yes, he didn't know it was a suicide vest. I told him to stand still for me and don't move. He didn't understand, but he was willing to do as I asked. He kept chattering to me about how wonderful his Uncle Mohammed was, and that he was going to be living with him from then on. He wanted to thank me for saving his life and to thank all the Americans for being his friend."

Jake pinched his nose, then finally continued. "I was as shocked as anyone when the bomb tech yelled to get back and dove as far as he could away from Hamal just a second before the vest exploded."

"Oh, Jake," Vidalia exclaimed, tears leaking down her face.

He gripped her hand. "I couldn't believe it," he said, his voice croaky. "I figured the bomb tech would take the suicide button away from Hamal and that would be it, but it didn't come with one. It was triggered remotely. Once they figured Hamal wasn't going to do any more damage than to the bomb tech, they set it off anyway. They had obviously been hoping for more, but the vigilant guard at the gate instantly recognized what was going on. He hadn't wanted to shoot Hamal, so he'd told him to stop."

"T-that is so wrong," Vidalia replied gruffly.

"I'm not telling you this for sympathy, Vidalia, I'm telling you because I know what it's like to blame yourself. I went over it a million times in my head, it drove me crazy. If I hadn't been so busy that day...if I hadn't yelled at him...if I'd just gone and apologized for yelling...and a thousand more ifs," he said wearily.

"How could you have known he would leave the camp," Vidalia protested. "It's not your fault, he knew he wasn't supposed to, right?"

He stared down at her. "He knew he wasn't supposed to, but children are unpredictable. You can't trust them to remember to do the right things when they are upset. And they are gullible and trusting of adults. We had insurgent patients recovering in another tent. Did he talk to one of them unsupervised? Convince him his family was waiting for him and he needed to go to them? Did he go into the desert alone because I was rough on him? I'll never know what prompted him to disobey me and the camp rules, but he did. And I felt responsible because I'd saved his life."

"What did you do?" She asked, her heart aching for him.

"I was forced into debriefing there because I couldn't get out of it," he replied. "But it didn't really help me. I spent three more months living in hell, and when my tour was up, I didn't stay. I ran. When I got home, my dad realized what was happening to me and he got me into therapy. Against my wishes, I might add, but I went. And I worked on my cabin. And I hiked to Fairy Lake every day, sometimes twice a day."

"Do you still blame yourself?" She whispered.

He sighed. "I suppose I'll always blame myself for part of what happened to Hamal, but I learned to forgive myself for my part in it. Even if I hadn't yelled at him, it still might have happened. But it took someone else guiding me through the landmines that finally helped me heal. I was like you, headed down a giant rabbit hole that was threatening to swallow me up. I couldn't live like that."

Vidalia was silent, absorbing the things he'd told her. She'd been running too, as fast as she could go. Perhaps it was time for her to concentrate on healing. "Can we go to Fairy Lake tomorrow for coffee and the sunrise?"

"Of course," he replied, gazing down at her. "But if we're going to get there by sunrise, we need to get some sleep, I know you're exhausted. He laid back onto the pillows, pulling her down with him, then settled the blanket over them both.

Cocooned in Jake's warm strong arms, the last thing Vidalia remembered was staring into the fire and thinking about a little brown-eyed boy laughing and running around. For the first time in weeks, she felt safe and slept without nightmares.

Chapter 9

Over the next several days, Jake and Vidalia hiked to Fairy Lake and Victoria Falls at least once a day. Vidalia was hoping to see the bears at the falls again, but Jake was hoping they wouldn't. Not seeing them meant they'd left the area.

Except for one day when Vidalia had gone into town to do some shopping and he'd run a few errands and followed up on some phone calls he'd made, he'd stuck by her side and she'd finally accepted that he wasn't going away. And of course, he'd spent the night at her cabin for the last three nights again in spite of her taunting him about inviting himself over.

The ranger had come by Vidalia's cabin and she'd given him her signature, but hadn't made a decision on what to name the baby bear yet.

Jake wanted to get closer to Vidalia but she kept him at arm's length. Sitting at his desk and waiting for her, he opened his mail from Friday's maildrop. At last, the police report his buddy had promised him regarding the investigation into Dani's death was here.

It had taken some doing to get a copy of it, but he'd finally managed after calling Dani Owens's parents and explaining who he was and that he was trying to help Vidalia Minton. They had authorized the release of the paperwork. He read, not knowing what he was looking for, but something, anything that might help Vidalia let go of the blame she was carrying on her slender shoulders.

The exact area Dani's body was found was described and he knew it well. It was a treacherous ravine in good weather, let alone trying to race a flood of water out of it. What he found most interesting was the description of the items released back to the parents. One of them was a cell phone. It said the cell phone had been found on a ledge in the upper part of the canyon. Authorities had begun searching near the trail-head that was in the campground in which Dani and her family had camped. Which meant for some reason, Dani had somehow gotten lost and ended up in that ravine.

Jake frowned, wondering how in the world the parents had lost that little girl to begin with? According to the parents' statement, the mother's cell phone had been damaged and quit working when she'd bent over a hot pot of coffee on their campfire and the cell phone had slipped from her t-shirt pocket and into the hot boiling liquid. That had left them with only the father's phone. He grunted, making a mental note not to ever let that happen.

It went on to say that Dani loved to take pictures and they had allowed her to use her father's cell phone for a little while with the caution to stay close, but then when they had called her for dinner, she didn't appear. Frantic they had begun looking and calling for her, but a storm was moving in. The father had raced to the nearest campsite and borrowed a phone to call for help while the rest of the family had stayed in camp in case Dani returned.

Jake frowned. When Dani had gotten lost, she knew her mother's cell wasn't working, and she knew to call 911 for emergencies, so that's how she had ended up connected to Vidalia. How in the world, if Dani's body had been washed to the bottom of the ravine, had the cell phone managed to stay on a ledge? It should have gone with her or been lost in the mud and rocks on the bottom after the flood washed through. An idea began in his mind. If he was right, he might be able to bring Vidalia some relief and help her forgive herself. When she pulled up front, he went to meet her.

Opening the door, he invited her in. "Do you need to use the bathroom before we take off?" he asked, pouring coffee into his thermos. Briskly he stuffed the whole thing in his backpack along with some snacks and some rocky road fudge. If he was right, this would be a day to celebrate.

"I'm ready, I just went at my cabin," she protested with a laugh. "We're just headed to Fairy Lake. Besides, you know I can pee behind a tree if I have to," she teased.

"Don't remind me," he mocked, his eyes glinting with good humor. "Seeing your naked butt sticking out from behind a tree is far too tempting. It needed to be a nice shade of pink for not going before we left."

She laughed then, and he was reminded of how good that sounded. "Come on, I have a surprise for you today."

"We aren't going to Fairy Lake?" she complained wistfully, her eyebrows lifting. "I was getting used to that. I really like it there."

"We'll go again, I promise," he replied, leaning forward and planting a buss on her forehead. Then turning her around and landing a spank on her backside, he pushed her forward. "Let's go."

"Okay, 1870," she drawled. "You really need to stop doing that."

Since she wasn't complaining too loud, Jake figured she didn't really mind. Although the 1870 always amused him. "You need it, what else can I do?"

It was about 12 miles over the pass and down the other side of the canyon they were in when Jake finally pulled into a campground and wound towards the back area. They had both been silent for whatever reason. Maybe it was his tense aura that had her sneaking side eyes at him as they drove, he didn't know. It wasn't an awkward silence though, just one that two people who were comfortable with each other could enjoy and not feel like they had to talk all the time.

"What's here? Another trail?" she asked when he drove towards a trailhead sign. When they got close enough, she gasped and looked over at him. "Rangers Pass?"

He put the truck in park and caught her hand. "Do you still want to go?" He asked quietly. It's about like the Fairy Lake trip, an hour and a half down and then back up."

"So, a three-hour round trip," she said, her voice croaky. She cleared her throat and then nodded. "Yeah, I want to go."

They gathered their gear and got out of the truck. At the trailhead sign, there was a warning beneath the white lettering of the name.

Warning! Do not attempt this hike in inclement weather. Canyon is prone to flash flooding.

Vidalia sucked in her breath. Had Dani read the warning? If so, how could she have ended up on this trail? She stared up at Jake.

Jake knew exactly what she was thinking, he was thinking the same thing. As they started down, Jake shared what he'd read in the police report. "So, what I'm wanting to do is find that ledge and try to figure out why Dani wasn't on it."

Vidalia didn't say anything else until she paused for a breather at a spot that wasn't loose shale. "What you've told me all makes sense," she replied slowly. "I've been thinking about it and remembering our conversation. Dani told me there were some roots sticking out above her but she was so cold she could barely move. Right after that there was a lighting burst in the background and I couldn't hear her reply. Then there was just the sound of rushing water and the phone went dead."

Jake nodded. "Okay, so let's add tree roots into the equation. He pointed to the sides of the ravine that were slowly coming closer together. From this point on, it would have been a lot harder to avoid the water. You can see the water marks from years of flash flooding on the rocks," he said. "We know the phone had to be above those marks, on a ledge, or it would have been swept away. Plus, the report said it was found tangled in a small shrub."

"We are already 30 minutes from the campground. How could Dani have gotten so turned around?" Vidalia asked with a frown.

Jake sighed heavily. "I can't answer that, but let's keep looking."

Another thirty minutes into their downward trek and they found it. "That has to be it," Vidalia exclaimed. "Look! Exposed tree roots and a ledge just above the base."

"You could be right," Jake replied. "At this point the water at its highest peak would have been over Dani's head. Unless she could get higher, she would have been swept away. That ledge could hold her if she could have gotten to it."

Vidalia shook her head. "Dani didn't even try," she croaked. "She was too scared. This is why I blame myself. I should have been able to convince her."

"Then how did the phone get on the ledge?" Jake asked, his eyes gleaming down at her. This was the thought that had been eating at him ever since he'd read that report.

Vidalia's mouth dropped open and she was at a loss for words. Finally, she stuttered, "S-she must have thrown it up there."

His eyebrow rose. "And lose her connection to you? You were the only thing she had in that moment. With you, she wasn't alone."

"Oh god, Jake," she whispered, sinking to the ground. "Do you think she actually tried?"

Jake grabbed hold of the tree roots. Some of them fell away in his hand when he tugged on them, but others held. "I think she tried," he replied, showing her the thin tendrils in his hand. "I really think she tried, but either her hands were too cold to hold the roots, or they broke off when she tried to climb so she fell all the way in. Once she was in the water, she couldn't get out and she was swept away, leaving the phone behind. With that downpour, I'm sure it died pretty quickly."

He stepped up on the soft ground where he was able to see the top of the ledge. "There's some brush growing on this ledge and I bet that's what kept the cell phone in place when the rain was beating down on it. That kept it from sliding off the ledge." He stepped back down and looked at her. Then he hunkered down in front of her and took her hands. They were cold and trembling. "It wasn't your fault, honey. You have to believe that she tried to get to safety because you were helping her."

Vidalia's eyes were green pools with tears leaking from them. "It beats the hell out of the alternative," she sobbed brokenly.

Jake sat down beside her and pulled her into his chest. "Oh, honey, have faith in yourself."

"Either way, she's dead, Jake," she cried. "And that really *really* hurts."

Jake pulled Vidalia into his lap and held her, the sobs wracking her slender body until she couldn't cry anymore. It took a while. Finally, she lay silent and still against his chest while he rubbed her back. It wouldn't be the last time she cried for Dani Owens, he knew, but at least she was finally grieving.

"I think I need to pee," she finally said, trying to get up.

He chuckled and stood up, helping her up with him. "Leave it to you," he teased.

Vidalia wrapped her arms around his waist, surprising him. "Thank you, Jake. You've really helped and I appreciate the trouble you've gone to on my account." She reached up and kissed the bottom of his chin, her watery smile peeking through.

"At last," Jake growled and swooped down to take her lips in a gentle plunder, his heart rate skyrocketing. "I didn't think you were ever going to kiss me first." Then he did it all over again.

Finally, Vidalia pulled away, her eyes leaking again. "Let's finish this," she said quietly. Taking his hand, they started down the ravine together, Vidalia pausing every now and then as something caught her eye. When they reached the bottom, she stopped as the trail flattened out and eventually ended near a parking lot of a lower campground. He wondered what she was thinking as she stared off into the horizon.

"Let's have a drink and a snack before we head back," he said quietly, gently tugging her toward a nearby picnic table. Without a word she allowed him to lead her to the bench where they sat down.

"There is one more thing," Jake said after they ate some snacks and drank some water. "You don't have to do it if you don't want to. It's just an option."

She looked over at him. "What?"

Jake studied her face closely. She was quiet, pale, but no signs of zoning out. Satisfied, he went on. "I took the liberty of looking up Dani's parents. They would like to meet you—if you're willing."

Vidalia's eyes widened. "Why would they want to? They must surely hate me, especially with all the news reports and the lousy stories being regurgitated about reckless and irresponsible dispatchers at that time. I'm not sure I can take their censure, Jake." Her lips trembled and she bit her lower one trying to control her feelings.

Jake shook his head. "I don't think so, honey. Her mother broke down and asked me to tell you she would dearly like to meet you, and that she knew you'd done everything you could to help her little girl. She wanted to thank you in person. She wanted to reach out and make contact before, but the police told her it wouldn't be a good idea, and the emergency center protected you from contact. She couldn't reach you."

Vidalia closed her eyes as yet more tears leaked down her face. "When?" she asked throatily.

"Today—if you want. I can call her right now, they are waiting for your decision."

"Why did you wait until now to tell me? I'm not prepared."

The anguish in her voice stirred a deep chord in Jake. He never got the kind of closure with Hamal that Vidalia was being offered with Dani. To the family of Hamal, he was the enemy. The enemy of all their family members. Nothing he could say or do would ever change that.

"I didn't want you to worry about it," he finally admitted. "Knowing in advance would keep you on edge and upset."

"You're right about that," she agreed with a heavy sigh. "Make the call, Jake, I'd like to meet them too. I wanted to go to the funeral and pay my respects, but my boss said it wouldn't be a good idea. Now is my chance to tell her how sorry I am that she lost her child," she added gruffly.

Jake couldn't have been prouder of his girl as he picked up the phone.

VIDALIA TOOK A DEEP breath after Jake helped her out of the truck and just stood there staring at the suburban home that belonged to the family of Dani Owens.

"You ready?" Jake asked, taking her hand.

She stared up at the man who had made this possible and nodded. Her eyes were glued on the front door as they slowly walked up the sidewalk towards the ranch-style home of tanned brick and partial wood.

It was neatly landscaped with spring daffodils and crocus peeking their heads through a redwood mulch in front of the concrete porch. The lawn was neatly trimmed and the spacious subdivision property had some large trees in the back yard that stretched high into the sky.

It was a typical family home in an influential neighborhood complete with a fenced-in backyard and a cat on the front steps. Brightly colored cushions adorned the rattan patio bench setting in front of the window with a wrought-iron white drink table to add to the ambience. Even a couple of beautiful Adirondack chairs set on either side of the bench, their sandalwood coloring blending in. It looked inviting and warm.

Vidalia's insides were feeling wobbly as Jake rang the doorbell. She held her breath when the door opened and she came face to face with Dani's mother. Almost sick to her stomach, she waited for Barbara Owen's reaction, praying that she wouldn't suddenly lay into her with horrible accusations, or worse yet, a silent hatred in her eyes.

"Vidalia?" The soft-spoken woman opened the outer door, her big blue eyes so like her daughters, filling with tears. "I'm glad you came. Please, come inside."

She reached forward and grabbed Vidalia's hands while Jake grabbed the screen door and held it so they could step up and into the house. Vidalia's own eyes watered when Barbara engulfed her in a gentle hug, her slender body trembling and warm against her. It should have been an awkward moment, but Barbara wouldn't allow it to be.

"Come in and meet my husband, Clay."

"We're happy you agreed to see us, Vidalia," Clay said gruffly, putting his arm around his wife. He nodded at Jake. "Thank you for bringing her to see us."

Vidalia was almost overcome with emotion. "I-I wanted to tell you how sorry I was about Dani before this, but..."

"I know, dear," Barbara replied, taking her hand and finishing her sentence. "It was inappropriate. They told me the same thing."

Vidalia nodded mutely, a lump in her throat.

"I want to show you something," Barbara said gently. She led them both through the spacious living room and into a separate dining room with a sunny, patio window where there were some photographs laid out on the table. She sat down in one of the cushioned dining chairs and pulled Vidalia down into the one next to her. Jake and Clay sat down on the ends of the table and leaned forward.

Clay cleared his throat, then spoke. "After the police returned my cell phone, I was able to dry it out and get the pictures off it that Dani took."

Barbara nodded. "My little girl loved animals. We were going to get her a camera for her birthday so she could take all the photographs she wanted. Every time we went camping, she always wanted to use our cell phone and take random pictures of anything that took her fancy, but mostly she loved animals," she explained, her voice cracking slightly.

Clay chimed in again. "We believe we figured out why Dani wandered away," he said gruffly. He pointed to some photographs directly in front of me. "Look closely at those pictures. Can you see them?"

Vidalia bent over the photographs, studying them intently. There were photos of what looked like animal tracks, a bird in the bushes, some spring mountain flowers peeking up and some pretty rocks. But when she gazed closely at the two in the middle, she suddenly gasped. "Those are bears near the ridge," she blurted out. "Look, Jake, it's the mama bear and her cub!"

Jake leaned in and took one of the photographs. "You're right," he exclaimed. Even with the camera zoomed in as far as it will go, it's still a distant shot, but it's certainly bears."

"Do you think it could be our bears?" she asked, her eyes shining with excitement.

"Your bears?"

"What bears?"

Barbara and her husband both chimed in at the same time.

"I'm amazed that she was able to spot them," Jake replied. "Dani has a good eye for photography.

"I saw bears on my hike to Victoria Falls, Vidalia replied in answer to their questions. See?" She showed them the pictures of the mama and cub that she had taken on her phone camera. "I bet you're right about why Dani kept getting further away from camp, she was trying to get better shots. She must have been thrilled and excited."

Barbara nodded, her eyes tearing up again. "There is one more thing. For some reason, the cell phone call had been set to record during her call to 911. Probably because Dani was fascinated with that aspect of the phone. She was smart and loved electronics. For only being eight years old, she had an amazing understanding of how to work all sorts of things. She could work the TV remote better than I could," she said fondly, sniffling.

Vidalia's mouth was dry. "S-she recorded it? You've listened to the tape?" Oh god, this was where they started yelling at her. She cringed and shrank back. "T-then you know I failed her," she stuttered. "I-I'm so sorry..." Her voice trailed off and she dropped her head unable to face the censure she knew must be coming.

Barbara lifted her chin and smiled. "I'd like to think Dani did this on purpose because she loved me and was scared she might not survive. I realize that's probably just a foolish mother's imagination, but either way, this tape has brought me such comfort; I've listened to it a thousand times. You were there for my little girl, every step of the way. She had someone to talk to and she wasn't alone. You can't know how much that means to me."

Her voice broke as she tried to hold back a sob. "I've wanted to thank you for so long. It's every mother's nightmare to imagine her child alone and scared with no one to turn to, but you were there, Vidalia. You didn't abandon her and you didn't stop trying to help her. The police said she must have been climbing on the roots when they gave way because they found root pieces in one of her hands, and one stuck in her t-shirt material."

"Oh my god," Vidalia whispered brokenly, tears suddenly overflowing. "She really did try, didn't she?"

Barbara nodded. "Yes, she did. And all because you were there and cared enough to do your job to the best of your ability. Thank God for dispatchers like you, Vidalia. Where would we all be without you?"

Vidalia would never forget the joy she felt in that moment as the burden of guilt lifted off her soul leaving her drained and spent. "You can't know what this means to me either," she whispered weakly.

Clay cleared his throat. "The parks department has finally approved our request to put a memorial bench near the top

of Rangers Pass for our daughter. We plan on having a candle-
light vigil there in memory of Dani. Would you like to come?"

Vidalia nodded, unable to speak. She reached out to Jake
and he took her hand and held it in his warm grip. Suddenly an
idea occurred to her and she found her voice, albeit croaking.
"Do you mind if we borrow one of the closer shots of the bears?
If the parks service can zoom in on the mother, they might be
able to tell if it's the same bear I saw. And if it is, that means
Dani is the first person to submit a shot of the new baby."

Barbara looked confused and Vidalia chuckled and sniffed.
"They've awarded me the honor of naming the baby bear since
mine is the first picture they've received. The mother's name is
Sushi, but if this is Sushi, then I think Dani should have the
honor of naming the baby. Do you have any idea what name
she might like?"

"Wait here," Barbara said, her eyes lighting up with excitement. She left the room and returned holding a stuffed black
bear. "We bought her this last year because she fell in love with
it when we visited a gift shop in Montana. She named him Buttons because of his black eyes." She smiled a sad little smile.

"Buttons, I love it," Vidalia said, taking the bear in her arms
and staring down at it. Then she smiled at Barbara. "It's perfect.
Sushi and Buttons."

"May I?" Jake asked picking up one of the photographs.
"We'll let you know if this is Sushi, but even if it's not, we'll find
out the name of this pair for you if it's possible."

"And I'm naming Sushi's cub Buttons in honor of Dani
anyway," Vidalia added with a smile. She handed the stuffed
bear back to Barbara and they spent the next hour visiting and
looking at photographs.

By the time Jake pulled up to Vidalia's cabin, she was yawning widely. They had stayed in town after visiting with the Owens's and gone to lunch then went to a local mall. Vidalia knew Jake was keeping her busy to keep her mind off things and she appreciated it. He'd even taken her out for Mexican food before they headed back to the canyon.

They sat there in the dark for a few minutes, the headlights spotlighting the steps up to the deck, the truck idling. She was exhausted. Finally, it occurred to her that he might be waiting for her to get out so he could leave. She frowned, not sure how she felt about that. Yeah, she'd been giving him flack for inviting himself over every night of her stay so far, but she'd gotten used to it, and now tonight he didn't seem inclined to stay.

"Thanks for today, Jake," she finally offered in the suddenly awkward silence. Come to think of it, he'd been strangely quiet after they'd left the Owen's home. She'd been so engrossed in her own emotions she'd barely noticed, but now she was remembering. Guilt swept over her.

"You're welcome," he replied quietly.

"Are you coming in?" she asked timidly, wondering if she'd gone so far as to actually offend him. Jake was hard to offend in her book, but he wasn't being his usual arrogant, take-charge self either. Or could it be that now he figured he'd solved all her problems he was ready to move on? Her heart clenched at that thought.

He turned to face her, His expression was guarded, his eyes dark in the moonlight. "Are you asking me in?"

She snorted then. "Since when do you need an invitation?"

He sighed and turned off the engine. "Come on, you're so tired your eye bags have bags. You need to rest."

"Well, that's flattering," she retorted, but she had a sneaking suspicion he was right. She opened the door and was sliding out of the truck when he came around to help her. When her toe caught on the edge of the step she tripped into his arms.

"How many times have I told you to let me help you?" He scolded. "That one step down is a long stretch for short legs."

"My legs aren't short," she sassed back. "I'm five foot five inches."

He grunted and took her hand to help her across the uneven ground in the dark and up the steps. Not even a friendly swat for her sass. Her heart sank further. Never in a million years would she have thought she'd miss it.

She hadn't left the porch light on because she hadn't thought they would be gone the entire day. They fit well together, his long arm around her waist and gripping her side in case she stumbled. She felt safe and protected. "Uh, thanks," she said breathlessly as they stopped in front of the door while she fished for the key in her pack.

Once she finally got the door open, she reached in to flip on the lights. "I'm going to shower and change my clothes," she muttered heading for the bathroom where she'd left her yoga pants and t-shirt this morning.

He grunted something non-committal and headed towards the kitchen. Probably to get a beer, she decided. Staring in the bathroom mirror she realized he was right. Her eye bags had bags. She looked like a real hag with red-rimmed eyes. "No wonder he didn't want to stay," she muttered. "I wouldn't want to stay with me either. I look like death warmed over."

As she stepped into the shower, her mind drifted over the day. Was there something else bothering Jake? Hamal perhaps?

She'd been pretty self-absorbed today, maybe she needed to re-think it.

Chapter 10

J ake popped the top of his beer and sat down on the couch. He hadn't been this focused on Hamal in a long time. The need to be alone, to hide away somewhere in a tight ball was overwhelming. The only thing that had kept him going was making sure Vidalia had her closure. Their situations were alike, and yet vastly different.

Glancing at his watch, he realized that it was too early for him to go to bed, he wouldn't be sleeping much tonight anyway. With a grunt he got up and started a fire. He needed to pull himself together because Vidalia was already sensing something was wrong. Given her empathetic personality, most likely she would be thinking it was her fault, although it wasn't.

He fished for the cell phone in his pocket and then remembered he didn't have service in Dax's cabin. He swore softly. He could have used a quick call to the therapist he'd remained friends with. Finally, he went to the storage room behind the kitchen and grabbed Dax's axe. Exercise was next on his list of coping skills.

Turning on all the lights on the deck, and even the overhead pole light that lit up the surrounding area, he went to the woodpile and slammed the axe into the base of the huge tree trunk where Dax split his logs. Then he grabbed the first log from the pile Dax had delivered a few weeks ago and set it on the base of the tree. Grabbing the axe, he began.

Steadily he worked in a rhythmic fashion, the release of pent-up emotional energy feeling good. It wasn't fifteen minutes before he shed his t-shirt and wiped the sweat from his face and brow before he began again. At some point, he was vaguely aware of Vidalia leaning against a pillar on the porch and watching him, but his focus was on the clean sweep of the axe that used his entire upper body. He didn't know how long he'd been out here before exhaustion began to creep in. The muscles in his arms trembled when he lifted the axe and he knew it was time to stop before he made a mistake and slipped or something.

Breathing hard, he slammed the axe into the tree trunk, grabbed his t-shirt and wiped his face and upper body. He needed a hot shower, but he was already feeling better.

Turning off the outside lights as he went, he stepped inside only to find Vidalia waiting for him. She slipped her slender arms around his waist and laid her head on his chest. The clean refreshing scent of her lavender shower wash drifted up his nostrils.

He stiffened. "I'm sweaty and dirty and you're clean, little girl," he said gruffly. "Why are you hugging me?" He put his arms around her in spite of himself. She felt good. He buried his nose in the top of her hair and inhaled, then laid his cheek on her warm head.

"Because I want to," she replied softly, not moving an inch.

Jake hugged her tightly like a drowning man clinging to a life raft. A few tears leaked from beneath his eyelids and slid into her soft hair. When her arms snaked their way up and around his neck and she lifted her mouth in offering, it was easy to let her tug his head down to kiss her.

His body tightened with pleasure as he plundered her soft mouth. Again, he tried to give her an out. "I need to get a shower," he said thickly against her lips.

"No, you don't," she replied, pulling him closer.

If they melted into each other any further, you wouldn't be able to sneak a piece of paper between them. He slid both his hands beneath her auburn locks and controlled her head, forcing her to look straight into his face where he could read her eyes and body language clearly. "Does this mean you're ready for a relationship? Or are you just feeling sorry for me?"

She cleared her throat. "I was ready for you the minute I saw you; I was just stubborn and wanted to do things my way," she replied, her heart in her eyes.

Jake groaned and was delighted at the same time. She really meant it; he could see that. "Remind me to spank your little butt for all the trouble you've caused me."

"Did I ever tell you that Trouble was my nickname when I was a child? My brother still calls me Trouble," she teased.

"I need to meet this family and get the low-down," he said. "You've probably got enough spankings earned to keep me busy for the rest of our lives."

"Hey, whoa, 1870. Just because I'm ready to spend time with you doesn't mean I'm ready to get married," she huffed.

He turned her around and landed a hard swat on her rear. "In that case, I'm going to get a shower. We can take up the subject of your indiscretions when I'm finished." His buddy below needed a cold shower.

She rubbed her butt and pouted at him. "There is such a thing as statute of limitations, you know."

Jake grabbed his pack with his clothes and grinned at her. "Not in my book." He dropped a quick kiss on her pouting lips and headed for the bathroom.

As Jake stood under the blissfully hot stream of water, he realized that Vidalia was good for him. The exercise had worn him out, but her warm body against his had brought the anxiety in his mind down to a manageable level once again. Not the case with his attraction to her though—that had ramped up one hundred percent.

They needed to talk about their formally new relationship, which *he'd* entered into a long time ago, and see where it led. He knew where he wanted it to go. The question was, did she want the same thing?

Once he was finished and dressed in clean sweats and a black t-shirt, he headed for the living room, his heart rate picking up. He stopped abruptly when he realized she was fast asleep on the couch. Ruefully, he shook his head.

As he studied the dark circles under her eyes, he knew she needed the rest. Technically, he needed to rest as well. Not wanting to disturb her, he grabbed a couple more blankets from her bedroom and a pillow, and made a bed on the plush rug in front of the couch. At least he could be near her.

Jake didn't know when it happened, but he awoke at one point during the night and realized that Vidalia was snuggled up next to him like a kitten seeking warmth, her arm thrown across his chest. He tugged the blanket off the couch and pulled it over both of them and drifted back off.

It was early in the morning when the pounding began on the front door, bringing Jake immediately awake. "What the hell?" He snarled as he jumped up.

"What's going on?" Vidalia asked breathlessly, jumping up with him.

"Let us in, let us in," yelled voices at the front door, the incessant pounding continuing.

Jake rushed swiftly to the door and moved the blind aside to see the two young men from Smokie's banging on the door and looking scared to death.

"Just a minute! Don't break the glass," he yelled back at them. He got the door quickly unlocked and opened it, the men stumbling in and huddling together.

"Close the door, she might be following us," Carrot Top shrieked.

Jake narrowed his eyes at him, but he closed and locked the door, then folded his arms across his chest. "What's this all about?"

"T-the bear with t-the cub," stuttered Dark Hair. "She broke through our patio door. We ran out the front door. She was s-still in our cabin when we left."

"We couldn't drive over because we don't leave keys in our car," added Carrot Top, "and we didn't think to grab them on the way out. We just wanted to get the hell out of there!"

"Where's your cabin?" Vidalia asked, her eyes wide and fearful.

"Not far from here, maybe a quarter of a mile," Carrot Top replied. "We came through the woods to get here."

"Did the bear follow you?" Jake asked, grabbing his backpack. "Come on, Vidalia," he directed, not waiting for them to answer him. "We're going to my house, it's more secure than these cabins. Plus, we have phone service."

"C-can we go with you?" Dark Hair ventured.

"Did you think I would leave you here?" Jake scowled impatiently as Vidalia hurried to his side. "Vidalia, the keys to the truck? It's safer than the jeep in case the bear is tracking these two."

Vidalia handed him the key and Jake opened the front door cautiously. It was quiet outside, nothing moving except a few ground squirrels running across the porch in the creeping dawn. "Let's go. If those squirrels aren't worried, we should be safe."

The two young men piled in the back seat while Jake and Vidalia climbed into the front. As they made their way along the lane to the main road, they didn't see a sign of the bears. Jake looked in the rearview mirror. "You wouldn't happen to be the idiots that were reported leaving food out in their trashcans, would you?"

They looked at each other and turned bright red. "We cleaned all that up after the ranger visited us," Carrot Top replied sheepishly.

"You're lucky," Jake retorted. "It's the bear that's unlucky. Now that she's tasted human food, she's coming back for more. You've caused a lot of trouble. I'm guessing the owner of that cabin won't be able to rent it out for the rest of the season either."

"What will happen to Sushi?" Vidalia asked. "They won't shoot her, will they? She has a cub."

"I don't know," Jake admitted. "We'll have to see what the ranger has to say."

Once inside Jake's home, he went to his office to make a call. His face was grim when he returned. "He's on his way now to the cabin."

Vidalia jumped up from the recliner. "What's he planning to do?"

"I didn't ask. But I told him the renters of that cabin were here with me, so we'll wait and find out."

"Can we borrow your phone?" Dark Hair asked tentatively. "We left ours in the cabin and I need to call our dad."

Vidalia's eyes widened. "Are you brothers? You don't look anything alike."

"We're adopted," Carrot Top replied sheepishly. "Dad isn't going to be happy about the cabin though. Especially since I'm guessing we'll be responsible for the repairs. He was going to join us for the weekend. We just came up ahead of him to do some hiking."

While the boys were using his office, Jake set about making some pancakes for breakfast. He always had pancake mix on hand, it was a quick fix. He threw some sausage links in a skillet to go with it, took some orange juice out of the fridge and called it good. "Breakfast on," he called to the three sitting in the living room where Vidalia was grilling them. She was worried about Sushi and Buttons, he could tell.

They were just finishing up their food on paper plates when Jake heard the rumble of a pickup truck pull up outside. He went to the door and managed to open it just as a huge man with a beefy fist raised stood there ready to knock. His brown eyes raked over Jake. The man had to be six-foot four and at least 275 pounds. His red checked flannel shirt didn't hold much of a belly either and Jake knew he'd be a mean customer in a fight.

"You got two knuckle heads in there that belong to me?" He growled.

"Dad!" The twin voices behind him rang out and the boys walked up as Jake moved aside, a sheepish look on their faces.

Jake almost felt sorry for the young men, but not completely. They were about to get a royal ass chewing if he was any judge of character, and they deserved it.

"I should bang your heads together," the man groused, but he stepped forward and put a large hand on each shoulder, his eyes roving them for damages in spite of his irritation. "Tell the man thank you for saving your puny asses and let's go see what the damages are."

Vidalia stood beside Jake as he received the boys' heartfelt thanks and huge handpump of a handshake from their father. "I'm beholden to you," he stated simply.

"You don't owe me anything," Jake replied with a grin.

"Don't be too hard on them," Vidalia piped up with a small smile.

"Oh, they'll be spending the summer repairing the damages to our cabin if I'm not mistaken," he boomed. "I just bought it too." He winked at her. "Insurance will cover it of course, but they'll work it off just the same."

"Well, welcome to the area," Jake replied with a grin. "They didn't say they owned the cabin. It looks like we are going to be neighbors. I'm Jake Bonner."

"That's because they don't own it, I do," The large man pumped Jake's hand again. "I'm pleased to meet you, Jake. I'm Marvin Feldman and these two scoundrels are Jason and John."

He pointed to Carrot Top and Dark Hair respectively. "If you have anything you need help with over the summer, you just call me. These two chowderheads will be delighted to help. Won't you boys?"

"Oh, sure,"

"Yeah, of course."

Both replies were mumbled and the boys flushed an even deeper red. "I'll remember that," Jake replied with a lazy grin. "I might have trees that need cutting down for firewood and a few other chores."

The boys looked panicked and their father chuckled. "That's good. They need to stay busy or they always find trouble." He scratched his head. "Or trouble finds them. I don't remember having that much trouble when I was seventeen, but then I might have some selective memory going on." He winked at Vidalia and Jake, then turned around. "Okay, haul it to the truck," he boomed, waving the boys out the door. "Let's get out of these folks' hair."

After they left, Jake turned to Vidalia. "Given that the parks department is out hunting for Sushi and Buttons, we probably shouldn't go hiking today, not until we hear from the ranger," he said.

She nodded. "And going back to my cabin, which is close to the epicenter, would be out of the question, right?" She sighed when he nodded. "I guess you're stuck with me then."

"I can't think of a better person to be stuck with," he drawled, sliding his arms around her and pulling her tight. "Maybe we can talk now, since we didn't get to last night." He took her hand and pulled her over to one of the recliners and sat down, then pulled her into his lap. So, Ms. Trouble, let's talk."

"Okay," she said with a grin. Then she dipped her head and started kissing him.

Rational thought went out of Jake's head until he heard the doorknob of his front door open and a gasp rip from a throat. Quickly he looked around Vidalia to see who had walked in without permission. "Mom—Dad—hi." Then he sighed. He really should start locking his door.

VIDALIA FELT THE RED creeping up her throat as she jumped off Jake's lap and nervously pushed her fall of auburn hair behind her ears. "Uh...hi," she said faintly, grateful when Jake stood up and put his arm possessively around her.

"Would you like us to come back later?" The woman asked with a broad grin.

"No. No—of course not," Jake hastily replied. "Come on in. I have someone I'd like you to meet anyway. He took her hand and walked over to his parents. "This is Vidalia Minton. Vidalia—these are my parents, Amelia and Steve.

Vidalia mentally groaned. Meeting the parents hadn't been on her list of things to do while she was here. Especially not when she was lip-locking with their son. Embarrassed, she nodded at them.

Jake looked like his dad, she decided. They had the same square jaw and gray smoky eyes. His dad was a little stockier than Jake but it wasn't a stretch to think he'd look like him one day, down to the silver streaks in the sides of his hairline. His eyes twinkled in approval as he studied her in return.

Amelia was a very pretty woman, her chocolate brown hair swept back in a ponytail up twisted into a bun. Curl tendrils bloomed along the front of her hairline, accenting wide, sky-blue eyes and a generous welcoming smile. She came forward and took Vidalia's hand. "It's a pleasure to meet you, Vidalia." Her contralto voice came out slightly husky but there was no denying her delight.

"And me too," Steve added, taking her hand from his wife. "It's a real pleasure to meet one of Jake's friends, and such a pretty one at that."

Vidalia blushed again. "Thank you," she replied, glad they seemed to approve of her. "It's a pleasure to meet you too."

Jake frowned. "You two aren't going hiking are you?"

"Actually, we are," Steve replied. We just came by to see if you wanted to hike up to Victoria Falls with us this morning and see if we can spot those bears everyone is talking about."

"Oh no," Vidalia gasped and shook her head.

"No, you don't want to do that today, Dad," Jake said. He went on to explain what had happened last night and what was going on today. "I'm guessing the trailheads around here will be closed right now while they look for Sushi."

"I hope they don't harm the bears," Vidalia added with a frown.

Amelia patted her shoulder. "Oh, don't worry about that, dear. As long as the bear hasn't attacked a person, they will try to catch her with a tranq gun and relocate her and the cub miles away from here."

Vidalia heaved a sigh of relief.

"Well, then I think I'll take your mother to lunch in the city, son. Would you two like to come along?" He asked glancing from her to his son.

She looked up at Jake and hoped he could read her stiff body language. His parents seemed lovely but she wasn't ready for that yet.

"No, thanks, Dad," Jake replied easily. "We haven't had a chance to jump in the shower and I know Vidalia won't go to town until she's gotten one." He looked down at her with a teasing glance. "We had to rush out of her cabin so fast last night she didn't even have time to bring any other clothes with her."

The glance his parents shot each other spoke volumes, but they didn't ask any nosy questions like what was Jake doing at her cabin in the early hours of the morning?

Vidalia nodded her head. She could feel the pink in her cheeks. "Another time maybe?"

Amelia grinned at her. "You can count on it."

After they left Vidalia groaned and dropped into the recliner. "I was so not ready for that."

Jake grinned down at her, his hands on his hips. "They like you."

"I hate to think about what *they* were thinking about," she confessed.

"Especially after they saw you had me pinned down in my chair," he teased.

"Oh you!" Vidalia threw one of the throw pillows at Jake.

Jake caught it and tossed it to the other chair. "Uh oh. Someone's being a naughty brat. Looks like she may need *daddy* to spank her bottom soon." He scooped her up from the chair shrieking and laughing and sat down with her on his lap where he proceeded to kiss her breathless. When he lifted his head he said firmly, "Relationship, right? Me boy, you girl, we date only each other?"

Vidalia laughed and then shyly nodded. "You're an idiot, but yes, I like that relationship."

"Calling names, another infraction," he warned, then started kissing her all over again.

Vidalia's senses were reeling. She wasn't even quite sure how she ended up flat on the rug trying to rip Jake's t-shirt off when the knock came on the door.

Jake groaned from the side of her neck. "Seriously?" He lifted himself off Vidalia and wrestled his t-shirt back in place, then ran his fingers through his hair.

Vidalia stared up at him through a half-lidded gaze. It wasn't until he grinned down at her and picked up her t-shirt and began twirling it around with his finger that she realized she was half-naked.

"Oh my god, give me that," she hissed, jumping up and grabbing it from his fingers while he chuckled. "You might want to head to the bathroom while I chase off whoever is at the door with a shotgun," he teased wickedly. He chuckled in pure male satisfaction as she ran for the bathroom, holding the front of her bra together.

Once inside the bathroom, Vidalia slammed and locked the door, panting from her manic run. Glancing in the mirror she almost didn't recognize herself. In awe she raised a finger to her swollen lips and touched her red, sensitive nipples. A shiver of rampant desire blazed through her. Even her pants were unsnapped and the zipper down.

Jake sure had skills—she'd give him that.

The haze of euphoria still held her in its grip, her lady parts aching to feel his strong fingers pleasuring her. She'd never used a toy before, but she'd give anything right now for the chance to try one out.

Groaning she turned on the cold water and splashed some on her face, then tried to smooth her hair down with trembling fingers. She was a mess. A thoroughly kissed, thoroughly turned-on mess that wanted nothing more than to pick up where they'd left off.

Quickly she got herself together and fished in her pocket for the hair tie she usually carried around with her in case she wanted to put her full, thick hair up in a ponytail or bun. She settled for a ponytail, at least it cut down on all the stray hair sticking out at odd angles. Feeling reasonably normal, she finally made her way back to the living room and spotted Jake with a man in a brown uniform with state parks insignias on it sitting at the table.

The ranger!

First impression was that he was younger than she'd thought he would be. Boyishly handsome, dirty blonde hair combed neatly in a short cut with pale blue eyes. He had muscles though, she could see that even through the uniform, although first glance would scream computer nerd.

"Did you catch the bears?" She asked breathlessly, sliding into one of the chairs at the table.

He nodded and smiled, eying her appreciatively. "You must be Vidalia."

She nodded eagerly.

"I'm Ranger Walker, and yes, we did. They are currently in transport to a remote location nowhere near any campgrounds or people," he said, his blue eyes twinkling. "I don't think we'll have any more problems with her, although bears have good memories."

Vidalia smiled back and heaved a sigh of relief. "That's good, I didn't want Buttons to lose his mother."

"Jake was telling me you'd decided on a name. I'm guessing it's Buttons?"

Vidalia looked at Jake. "Did you show him the picture?"

Jake shook his head. "I was waiting for you." He took the picture from his pocket that Dani's parents had given him and handed it the ranger. Then he and Vidalia took turns explaining where the name Buttons had come from and why.

Ranger Walker took the picture and stared at it. Then he took out his wallet and slipped a small magnifying glass out of a sleeve. After holding the picture under the glass, he grinned up at them. "This is Sushi all right. I can see the place on her ear that's torn. It was like that when we tagged her. The two sides of the ear healed by themselves and didn't grow back together."

Vidalia's throat filled up. "Then...then Dani really is the first person to photograph Sushi's first cub. That is all kinds of wonderful," she enthused. "Her parents will be so happy."

"She was an early bird this year," he marveled. "Little Dani got caught in that ravine about six weeks ago, and mothers with cubs don't usually appear that early."

Vidalia flinched at the comment but didn't say anything.

"Maybe something disturbed them," Jake chimed in.

"I'm sure something did," he agreed, "but we'll probably never know what it was." He stared at Vidalia's pale face and then his eyes softened. "You were the dispatcher on that call. Your name has been familiar to me since Jake called me but I couldn't place it until now. That's rough. I have a sister who is a 911 dispatcher. You people do a hell of a job. She's threatened to quit so many times. It takes a special person to live through other people's worst moments and come out sane."

Vidalia nodded, a lump in her throat. "We usually come out, but I don't know how many of us are ever the same again after some of the calls we take," she replied gruffly.

He nodded in sympathy, then held up the picture. "Do you mind if I have this picture? I'd like to make some prints of it and get her parents' authorization to use the photograph. Both photographs will be featured in the article with the new name."

Vidalia nodded and he stood up. "Well, I need to get going. Thanks for the calls and keeping us up to date on what's going on with the bears when you see something. Not everyone does and sometimes it doesn't end well for the bear."

Vidalia and Jake stood up and walked him to the door.

"Anytime we can help, just call," Jake said. "My parents and I both live here year-round unless there's a major weather hiccup. Then we head for lower ground."

"I would too if I had a cabin like this one," he enthused.

"It's a work in progress," Jake replied, pleased with the compliment.

After he was gone, Jake pulled Vidalia into his arms once again. "Now, where were we?"

"Um...we got about as far as me girl, you boy, we in a relationship," she replied with a giggle. "I don't remember much after that."

He shot her an aggrieved look. "I must be losing my touch if you can't remember."

She stood on her toes and planted a kiss on his chin. "Mostly I remember how I felt—and it was wonderful."

"Good to know." He kissed her deeply, his hands pushing up beneath her t-shirt to find the front of her bra once again. "Let's see if we can get back there."

Truck tires crunched on the gravel outside the front door and they both groaned. They waited with baited breath as heavy footsteps came onto the deck and clunked to a stop in front of the door. The next thing they heard was metal flipping onto metal and Jake heaved a sigh of relief.

"It's only the mailman."

Then came the knock on the door.

"Dammit," he swore softly and stepped behind her to yank open the front door.

Vidalia giggled at the look of surprise on the old man's face. His fist was still in mid knock, but he smiled quickly at Jake, his gray moustache lifting as his teeth appeared.

"Howdy, Jake. You have a package and I know you don't like me to leave them on the porch. He fumbled in his bag and brought out a cardboard box the size of a loaf of bread and handed it to him. Then he doffed his hat at Vidalia. "Ma'am," he said, and then turned around and went clunking off the deck and back to his huge truck.

"You didn't even say thank you," Vidalia chided with another giggle. "That poor man must have thought you really had a wild hair going on."

Jake's eyes narrowed at her. "Wild hair huh? I'll give you a wild hair."

Vidalia shrieked and ran as Jake chased her around the table and through the living room, finally catching her and swooping her up over his shoulder in a firemen's carry. Then he took her into his bedroom and dumped her on the bed and proceeded to tickle her until she screamed.

"Uncle! Uncle!"

He pulled her arms above her head and held them there while kissing her thoroughly. "I love it when you laugh," he purred, nuzzling the side of her face.

He allowed her to pull her arms down and she cupped his face in her hands and kissed him back. "Oh, Jake, I love it when you kiss me," she whispered.

Chapter 11

J ake moved over onto his elbow and ran his thumb down her lips. "You held out long enough."

"We've only known each other eight days, nine if you count the night I got to the cabin," she protested with a laugh.

He supposed it was a good thing they had been interrupted so many times in the living room because that really wasn't the way he wanted their first time together to play out. He wasn't sure Vidalia was really ready for that final commitment either, even though she'd given no indication of stopping him.

"You're right," he said, sitting up and pulling her up beside him. "Nine days isn't very long, although I know what I want. I just need you to know what you want for sure."

She searched his face with those incredible eyes of hers and then nodded. "Thank you," she said simply. Then she smiled. "One thing I do know I want is to go back to my cabin and get some clothes. They scurried for the truck before someone else could knock on Jake's door.

When they arrived at the cabin, Vidalia hit him with a sudden question. "Why were you chopping wood last night?" When he didn't answer right away, she put her hand on his arm. "Was it Hamal?" She asked softly.

He glanced over at her with a rueful smile. "Yeah. Sometimes I just can't sleep and exercise helps wear me out."

"Exorcises the demons, huh?"

"Something like that."

A worry line creased her smooth brow. "Jake, I really hope your efforts to help me aren't bringing you down. I can't imagine going what you went through and staying sane. I'm not sure I could recover from witnessing something like that first hand."

Her earnest words touched him. "Yeah, you can, that's why you're having so much difficulty—imagining it I mean." He palmed the side of her face. "Your empathy makes you vulnerable, which is what makes you so good at what you do. You just need to put some of that determination to help others into helping yourself."

"I will see someone when I'm done with my vacation, I promise." She gave him a mock salute.

His eyes narrowed. "I'm going to hold you to that promise, even if I have to spank your little butt all the way to your appointments."

"Okay, 1870," she retorted.

He chuckled. "Maybe I am old-fashioned, but I believe in taking care of my girl. And also, I can vouch from experience that you will learn coping skills that will help you, especially if you decide to keep your job. Or even if you don't and decide to be a nurse."

"Skills like going out half-naked and chopping wood?" she teased.

He leered at her. "Only if I'm there to watch."

"I don't think I have the muscles to do what you were doing," she replied, laughing. "I wouldn't look near as pagan in the moonlight as you did. That was awesome."

"I'm glad you liked what you saw," he drawled, leaning over and kissing her. She tasted delicious with the flavor of maple syrup clinging to her lips. Finally, he lifted his head and stared down into her bemused expression. "If you keep seducing me like this, we're never going to get any hiking in today."

Indignation replaced bemused. "Why...you...*you* kissed *me*," she accused, rolling her eyes and shaking her head.

He grinned unrepentantly. "I just can't resist you."

Vidalia blushed and rolled her eyes again. She yanked the truck door open and slid out, marching for the cabin.

Jake chuckled in satisfied amusement. His little onion had so many layers, he was really enjoying each one.

The following Thursday Jake received the call from the Owens that the memorial bench for Dani had been completed at the top of the trailhead for Rangers Pass. They had decided a bench had more meaning because it was a spot people could sit down and contemplate or just enjoy the silence and beauty of the mountain. She and Jake had hiked up there a few times to see how it was developing, but they hadn't seen the completed memorial.

Rangers Pass was eerie to Vidalia. She'd tried to get past the feeling, but couldn't help wondering how many people had lost their lives in that ravine in the past. To her it felt haunted. She was somber as she prepared to attend the vigil. Jake said it was an opportunity for closure, but she really wondered if she should go at all.

Ever since Saturday when she and Jake had tentatively decided to be a couple, they had spent almost every waking hour together. They started out in their own beds most nights in her cabin, but sometimes they ended up together in front of the fire-place on the couch if one or the other, or even both were having trouble sleeping.

Oftentimes they would just sit on the bench at Fairy Lake without speaking a word. As if sensing her need to be alone, sometimes Jake would hike on around the lake without her and throw in a fishing rod he usually carried in his pack. She could see him across the water and he would wave occasionally.

Those were the times her thoughts turned to her job—and Dani. Sometimes she would shed some tears. When she no longer wanted her own thoughts for company, she would hike around the lake and meet him. He never caught anything and she suspected he didn't even have any bait with him, but he fished just the same. He was clearly one of the good guys.

Jake was holding back with her, she knew that. Her feelings were mixed. Some days she wanted him so much she could barely stand it. Other times he wanted her so much he went out and chopped wood. She wasn't sure what he was waiting for, perhaps some unseen signal she had yet to give off?

Probably.

Down deep she knew she still wasn't ready for that change of focus from her pain and sorrow to developing a complete re-lationship. She sighed and stared at herself in the mirror, hop-ing he was right about attending this vigil.

Bemused, she realized she must have lost more weight than she'd thought. The long-sleeved forest green t-shirt she wore fit her more loosely than it used to. So did her dress jeans. The ca-sual white kerchief she'd knotted around her neck brought out the dark auburn cast of her hair while the shirt enhanced her wide green eyes. Her face was thinner too, making her eyes ap-pear even larger.

When Jake's handsome face appeared in the mirror behind her, she started. "Oh! I didn't hear you come in."

"You look gorgeous," he stated simply, his eyes roving her face. "You doing okay?"

She nodded. He looked gorgeous too. The lightweight sweater rested easily on defined muscles in his arms and hugged his impressive abs with a silky touch. He hadn't shaved and that dark shadow on his square jaw was sexy as hell with those smoky eyes and windswept dark hair looking like she'd run her fingers through it. Attraction rippled through her. She turned and rested her hands on his lean hips, then ran her fingers beneath the sweater loving the feel of the warm skin on his back.

He pulled her in close to his body and dropped his head to kiss her causing her senses to explode. Flattening herself against his hard body, she changed position and stretched up high to put her arms around his neck and rub her tingling breasts against his muscles. Then she was lost in a mind-numbing kiss. He pressed up against her, his rock-hard manhood straining against her abdomen making her wish it was lower.

Finally, he lifted his head and whispered against her lips. "You're driving me crazy, little onion. I want to peel you out of those clothes so bad right now that we better get going. It's not like I can chop wood if we're going to make it to the vigil."

Vidalia sighed. "Okay. Right now, I'd rather go to the vigil than watch you chop wood. That eye candy wouldn't make me feel any better either."

He turned her around and pushed her butt towards the door. "One of these days, I'm not going to resort to chopping wood."

She didn't answer and she wasn't sure why she didn't. What in the world was holding her back?

There weren't a lot of cars in the parking lot when they arrived, but then they hadn't expected there to be since Barbara had told her it was only close friends and family. She was grateful for Jake's sheltering arm around her as they made their way towards the small group of people gathered around the memorial. The circle opened quietly to include them and they got their first look at the completed bench.

Tears welled up in Vidalia's eyes. "Oh my gosh, it's so beautiful," she choked out. She reached out with a trembling finger and traced the outline of the mother bear and the cub that appeared to be walking in a row of pine trees etched into the metal of the back of the bench seat. The etched wording above the bears simply stated—*Dedicated to The Memory of Dani Owens.*

Quiet introductions were made and Vidalia and Jake shook hands and uncomfortably accepted hugs from various family members. Then Clay cleared his throat and handed everyone a candle. "The sun is setting, let's light our candle's and begin," he said. He lit his candle first and then leaned over and lit Barbara's with his, and so on all the way around the circle.

Vidalia listened as people took turns telling amusing/touching anecdotes about Dani and stared into the candle flame. No one seemed to expect her to say anything and she didn't want to, she was afraid she'd burst into tears or say something completely stupid and irrelevant. She did mourn for the loss of the little girl taken too soon.

After thirty minutes or so when people seemed to be winding down, Clay finished it up with a prayer giving Dani over to the care and keeping of the god they believed in. Once they blew out the candles, the only light in the area was from the tall telephone poles located at strategic areas around the perimeter.

"Thank you for coming, Vidalia," Barbara told her, enveloping her in another hug. "I hope you can find peace and let this go. Even though I don't know you very well, I can sense you've been holding onto Dani and blaming yourself. You have to let her go, she's fine where she is. It's hard..." Her voice broke and her lips trembled before she was able to collect herself and finish her sentence. "It's hard, I know that, but you're a strong young woman. Be good to yourself." She patted Vidalia's hand and then hugged Jake and left under the arm of her husband.

Vidalia nodded, unable to speak as tears leaked slowly down her smooth cheeks. She could hear people chatting softly and cars starting as people slowly left the area until only she and Jake were left. She shivered in the cool night air. Jake moved in and put his arms around her from the back, resting his chin on her head without saying a word. She knew he was waiting for her but she couldn't tear her gaze away from the bench.

"I...I want to sit there," she croaked, stepping forward and lowering herself to the cold metal of the unflinching bench. She spread her hands out beside her and touched it, feeling its smooth surface. Her gaze was suddenly drawn to the top of the trail where it headed down the pass and the hair on the back of her neck lifted. A shadowy image stood there looking over its shoulder at her, then with a smile, waved a small hand in the air and disappeared. Her eyes widened in disbelief.

"What's wrong," Jake asked with a frown, turning to stare at the trailhead.

"Do you believe in ghosts?" She asked, standing up.

"I believe there are things we don't understand," he finally replied. "Did you see something?"

"I-I think I saw Dani," she replied gazing up at him. "And she waved goodbye to me. Is that possible? Or am I officially off my rocker, as they say."

Jake chuckled and sat down to put his arm around her. "I've heard it said that sometimes when people are really suffering over a loss, they might see that person. But I don't know if it's true or not."

She shivered wondering if she really was losing her mind. "Have you ever seen Hamal?"

"Only in my dreams," he replied quietly. "I'll always remember the happiness on his face and his big brown eyes laughing at me. That's what I try to focus on when I'm troubled, and that's good enough for me."

"I feel finished here," Vidalia said quietly, rubbing the back of her arms. "I don't want to visit this place again anytime soon."

"Then let's go." He pulled her up and they went to the truck. Jake helped her into the tall seat, and as they drove away, she looked back one last time. There was nothing to see. "Goodbye, Dani," she whispered under her breath.

"What?" Jake asked, glancing sideways.

"Nothing. Let's go home," she replied, suddenly feeling like a weight had been lifted from her shoulders. Jake was right, coming to this vigil had been cathartic, if somewhat eerie.

"Yours or mine?"

"Yours, I think," she replied, her eyes shining up at him.

They were both silent as Jake drove down the canyon and parked in front of his cabin. It was a comfortable silence though, with Vidalia tucked warmly up beneath his protective arm as they made their way quietly inside.

"Would you like something to drink?" he asked as they came into the house.

She shook her head. "No, thanks."

He led her towards the couch. "Want to watch a movie?"

She stopped him with her hand on his arm. "No, I only want one thing."

His eyes glittered down at her. "And what's that?"

"You," she said simply, and reached for his face with her hands to pull him down for a kiss. He kissed her back and Vidalia finally understood what a toe-curling kiss was like. It was all consuming, sending darts of passion and pleasure to every nerve ending. His large hands came down and cupped her buttocks, lifting her against him as his teeth nipped her nipples now standing erect through the silky fabric of her shirt. Electricity sparked in her abdomen causing her to gasp for breath as she locked her legs around him, aching for his hardness to touch her there.

"I'm not sure I can stop if we don't stop now," he said thickly, lifting his head to lock gazes with her.

She bucked her abdomen, feeling for his hardness. "I don't want to stop."

His face hardened. "You realize this won't end with just a good girl spanking, right?"

"It better not," she taunted, "or I'll be pretty disappointed." She leaned down and kissed him. "I want you, Jake, all of you, and I want it now."

JAKE GROANED IN SURRENDER and carried her to his bedroom where he kicked the door shut behind him. "No interruptions this time," he vowed fiercely, setting his long-awaited prize on her feet.

In no time at all he had her stripped and laying on the bed in a pool of moonlight. "You're the pagan goddess now," he murmured, his eyes feasting on her gleaming skin. "So wild and beautiful."

He knelt beside her on the bed and began to explore the lush treats laid out before him. He took his time, relishing every gasp and moan as he ravished her mouth, nipped nipples and lathed them with his tongue, and massaged his way down her body until she was shaking and moaning with desire. "Open," he demanded as he moved down between her thighs.

"Jake," she moaned spreading her legs like petals from a flower opening up. It was poetry in motion as the gorgeous hidden rose bloomed in front of him.

"So frickin' beautiful," he muttered and then took his first taste. Desire shot through him like a thunderbolt, hardening him so hard he felt ready to burst. He wouldn't allow himself the ultimate pleasure though, until she was primed and ready for him. He lowered his head again.

"Oh—oh!" she wailed as if she was in pain and bucked against him, her body begging for more.

He gave it to her, tasting, licking and nipping until her legs stiffened and she screamed as the force of her pleasure overtook her. When she finally grew limp, he started licking his way back up her body, stirring those smoldering embers still burning inside her back to life. When he reached her breasts, he nipped her tender buds lightly, causing her to jump. "Is this your first time?" he growled hoarsely.

"No," she gasped, writhing beneath him. "I'm n-not a virgin if that's what you mean."

"Then up on your knees," he demanded, helping her turn over and positioning that beautiful ass right in front of him. Reaching into the drawer by the bed, he didn't waste any time slipping the silken sheath over his rock-hard rod.

She was trembling when he began spanking her lightly, rubbing his sheath against the wetness dripping down her legs. "Are you a good girl?" He crooned over her, reaching under one side to pinch her nipples.

"Yes...yes," she gasped. "I've been a good girl." She hesitated, then pronounced a word that seemed to make him even harder if that was possible. "*Daddy.*"

He sort of knew what the daddy stuff was all about, but hadn't given it much thought before. If she liked it though, he was more than willing to go with the flow. Hell, he was willing to explore anything—for the most part.

When her cheeks were nice and pink, he slowly slid into her from behind, easing his way into the hilt. When she began rocking back against him, he began thrusting harder and harder into her until she suddenly tightened, squeezing him inside and driving him mad with pleasure. He barely held on until she began a keening wail and began bucking. He didn't know if this was anything like riding a bucking bronco but it was the most fantastic thing he'd ever felt with a woman. His own release came so hard he could swear he saw stars, and he literally held her hips up with her face planted in the quilt until every last drop was milked. Then he collapsed with her, rolling to the side and breathing hard.

They lay there panting in the moonlight, their bodies so spent that Jake didn't even want to get up and get rid of the condom. Finally, he forced himself up but she grabbed his arm.

"Where are you going?" She asked with a yawn.

"I'll be right back, honey," he replied softly. Quickly he disposed of the sheath and washed himself off, then took a warm washcloth back to the bed and gently washed between her legs. She barely stirred.

When he returned to the bed, he lifted her legs and pulled the quilt down below her bottom and crawled in beside her, then covered them both up. She turned slightly and snuggled into his shoulder and draped her arm across his chest. "That was fantastic," she whispered.

"You were amazing," he growled, "so freakin' gorgeous." She fit him perfectly, Jake thought in wonder. His fingers trailed down the softness of her arm, marveling at the silky texture. Pulling her in close and kissing the top of her head, he relaxed and fell into a dreamless sleep. One of the few he'd had in several long months.

SOMETHING WAS POKING Vidalia in her bottom, something hard and insistent. With a sleepy yawn she peeked out through slitted lids. It was still dark outside. And then it came rushing back. She was in bed with Jake and it was the morning after the most fabulous lovemaking she'd ever experienced. Not that there had been many—okay—only two. And they hadn't been noteworthy.

Instant recognition blazed into her mind and she pushed back against that hard rod seeking entrance. A large palm slipped under her arm and cupped her breast, teasing a tender bud between thumb and forefinger while firm lips began kissing the side of her neck.

"Jake," she breathed, leaning forward slightly to allow him better access. Her body was already damp and she shivered, desire prickling along every inch of her.

"Good morning, beautiful," he husked in her ear.

"It's even better now," she replied with a gasp as he found his target and slipped in and out, creating even more slippery conditions. "Oh, that feels so good," she moaned.

Her butt was actually a little sore from the spanking, she realized as his speed increased and he pushed deeper into her. When his hand left her breast and his fingers slipped down and rubbed across the top of her already engorged bud, she shuddered. It was a deadly combination and one she couldn't resist—didn't want to resist. She reached for, and was rewarded with, another lovely ride among the stars.

They lay connected and she wanted to always stay this way. If the world and all its ugliness would go away, she and Jake would be just fine, just like this.

"You need to get up, little onion," he whispered into her ear. "We are going to have coffee and sunrise at Fairy Lake this morning."

"What time is it?" she groaned, giving into the inevitable as he got up and turned her over, then leaned down to plant a kiss on her lips.

"It's 4:00 am. We have just enough time for a quick shower and to grab some breakfast sandwiches in the microwave. We can eat on our way to the trailhead."

He was excited about something, she realized as she studied his face. He must have something special he wanted her to see, although she thought he'd showed her everything there was to see about Fairy Lake since they had been there many times over these last two weeks. "Okay," she replied with a smile.

They slipped into the shower together, grabbed their sandwiches, a thermos of coffee, and some bottles of water, and they were off. In Dax's truck, she realized ruefully. She might owe him some gas money or something after all the miles she'd put on it. "Did you sleep well last night," she asked, snuggling up against him on the seat.

"Like a log. How about you?" He glanced down at her with a smile.

"I slept great," she confessed, coloring slightly.

He gave a knowing chuckle and squeezed the hand he was holding.

Vidalia practically knew the trail by heart. The moon was a three-quarter moon, so total darkness wasn't a problem. By the time they reached their bench, the first rays of dawn were creeping across the sky. They sat down and Vidalia took the cups out of her pack and reached for the thermos, but Jake didn't hand her the thermos. Instead, he took something out of his pack and then dropped to his knee on the ground in front of her.

Realizing where this was going, her heart leapt into her throat and she instantly teared up. "Oh god, Jake," she choked out, trying to brush the tears away so she could see his face.

Opening up the black box between his fingers, the sun caught the sparkle of a single diamond set in a golden band, the prism of colors showing off the richness of its beauty.

"Vidalia Minton, will you marry me?" He asked softly. "I know it's early, but I think I've loved you from the first moment you sassed me with that beautiful mouth. I can't even imagine my life anymore without you in it."

"Oh, Jake," she cried softly, tears running down her face. So many things flitted through her mind. She'd thought she was too full of sorrow to even begin a relationship, but she'd come to realize instead of full, she'd been empty. A huge black hole had invaded her mind and no matter which way she'd writhed away from it, the darkness had kept following her. Jake had stood between her and the depths of that darkness since the beginning, and finally replaced it with himself. She didn't even know how to tell him how much she loved him.

He looked slightly uncomfortable with her silence. "If you aren't ready, I can wait until you are."

She held out her trembling hand to him, her heart in her eyes. "I'm ready. Now and forever, Jake. I love you seems inadequate for the way I feel right now."

Delighted, and with his own hand shaking, he took the ring out of the box and slid it onto her finger. Then he stood up and yelled "Yes! She said yes!" He grabbed her up and twirled her around in a circle, then let her slide slowly down his body while he kissed her senseless.

At last, they cuddled together on the bench he'd carved with his own hands, the one they'd spent many hours on contemplating the cruelties of life and their part in it over the last few weeks. It had brought them together and Vidalia could only think of only one place better to be. "The only place better than this is in your bed," she said wickedly, shooting him a side glance.

The sun was breaking full force above the majestic pines and dancing on the water lilies with their delicate flowers, making everything sparkle. Jake raised his coffee cup to hers. "From your lips to my ears," he said with a chuckle. "I'll do my best to keep it that way."

Vidalia tipped her cup into his and smiled in satisfaction. "So will I," she replied with a fervent promise. "I love you, Jake."

"I love you too, little girl."

She ran her tongue across her lips. "About that little girl thing..."

He placed a thumb where her tongue had been. "We'll peel away all your layers one by one, little onion. *Daddy,* has you covered on anything you want to try." He gazed down at her with a knowing grin.

She could see he really meant it. There were layers to her that she'd wanted to explore but hadn't had anyone to explore them with. "Okay," she agreed breathlessly.

Then he dropped his head and proceeded to kiss her senseless once again. "Promise we'll always come back here," she sighed, snuggling under his long arm as the peace and majesty of the morning settled on them like the soothing balm it was.

"Wild bears couldn't keep me away," Jake promised as he kissed the top of her head.

The horrific tragedies they had both endured would always remain a part of them because they had helped to shape who they now were. But with acceptance came a measure of peace, forgiveness, and self-awareness. Support, love, and time would take care of the rest.

For both of them.

The End

Don't miss out!

Visit the website below and you can sign up to receive emails whenever Brandy Golden publishes a new book. There's no charge and no obligation.

https://books2read.com/r/B-A-ZXWM-LFIFC

BOOKS 2 READ

Connecting independent readers to independent writers.

Did you love *Protecting Vidalia*? Then you should read *Achilles' Earth Angel* by Brandy Golden!

She kicked him in his weak tendon....she'd pay for that!One glance was all it took for the mighty god-like Achilles to fall hard for Ange Galanos. But the defiant, *not-so-angelic* little mortal he'd saved was turning his world upside down.Just the same, he had to have her!The only snag was Zeus, the king of the Olympians, and his decree of no contact with the human world.Would the penalty for defying Zeus' mandate be too high to keep his defiant little earth angel?

Read more at https://brandygolden.com/.

Also by Brandy Golden

Brocton Chronicles
A Shotgun Wedding

East Coast Spitfires
Taming His Irish Spitfire
Taming His Feisty Kitten
Taming the Wind

The Brocton Chronicles Book 1
The Maddie Stories

Standalone
Marlie's Christmas Keeper
Catching His Snow Bunny
Hot Little Firecrackers
Protecting Vidalia

Watch for more at https://brandygolden.com/.

About the Author

I'm a writer of compelling romantic stories in all settings. I love the American west cowboys, the Highlanders of Scotland, and the spitfires of contemporary romance.

My stories will always have strong males who don't mind turning a feisty young woman over their knee if the occasion warrants it. Sweet heat and passion, combined with some discipline make these stories of any genre captivating and enjoyable.

I live in the midwestern United States with a loving husband, five children, and five grandchildren, plus 3 furbabies. I also enjoy gardening scrapbooking, and of course, reading. Especially romance!

What you won't find in my stories is excessive foul language, overly descriptive and detailed sex, or BDSM. Well, mostly no BDSM. I do have a hint of it here and there, but I have talented friends who write that very well.

No, I'm more a fun-loving, John Wayne-style romance writer with just enough spanky spice to sizzle and keep you glued to the pages.

Enjoy the glow of romance, my friends, it's all around us..

Brandy

Read more at https://brandygolden.com/.

About the Publisher

In 2020, I finally got my opportunity to go independent in publishing my books. This is a journey I'm enjoying so far, and I hope you are enjoying my creations. Thank you for purchasing from Brandy Golden Books